I0547752

DELECTUS MORBIDIUM

Twenty unsettling tales

Merita King

Published by Merita King
Eastleigh
Hampshire
United Kingdom
© Merita King 2013 All rights reserved

Cover art by Joseph Brady and JL Stratton copyright 2013

Delectus Morbidium

ISBN 978-0-9570520-8-6

OTHER WORKS BY MERITA KING

The Lilean Chronicles: Book One ~ Redemption
The Lilean Chronicles: Book Two ~ The Sleeping
The Lilean Chronicles: Book Three ~ Changing Faces
The Lilean Chronicles: Book Four ~ Avalanche Effect

Floxham Island ~ Sinclair V-Log AZ267/M
Bygora Vandos ~ Sinclair V-Log LB734/A
Acts of Life

ABOUT THE AUTHOR

Merita King has loved the science fiction and fantasy genre in both books and movies since she was a young child. She has been greatly inspired by years of watching movies and reading books and has wanted to make a contribution to this genre for many years. Her stories all contain a strong spiritual thread as she believes that spirituality is universal and crosses all boundaries. She believes that the creative process is largely intuitive and can be very effectively blocked by too much pre-planning. "Plot lines, characters and events all come to me intuitively," she says, "and this makes the act of writing a constant pleasure." She is a psychic medium and lives alone in Hampshire, UK.

DEDICATION

This collection of unsettling stories is dedicated to all those of my friends and fans who so bravely volunteered to take starring roles. Without these wonderful friends, I would not have so varied a collection of murderers, crazies and innocent victims with which to delight, shock and unsettle.

Susan McGregor, Cody Martin, Tracey Gore, Lesley Hazelhurst, Rebecca Brockman, Rob Leggett, Donna Spencer, Brian Bigelow, Sheryl Galzote, Tracey Tabor, Rebecca Brown, Beverlee Ruhland, Emma Raby, Mandy Ward, Rob Clague,, David-John McVie, Theresa O'Neill, Mark Lewis, Brandy Edwards, Mike Wall, Jeany Williamson, Linda Sloan-Whitten, Santosh Kumar, Hannah Tate, Steve Pannel, Sood Saab, Omar Al Farsi, Sherry Smith, Diane Lira, Debb Levoie, Amanda Heath, Fiona McVie, Loreen Smallwood, Mark Morris, Sharon Rowe.

CONTENTS

A PICTURE OF FEAR
starring Susan McGregor

Susan stretched forward, the poster held at both corners and yelped as the chair upon which she balanced, wobbled. She held her breath and tried again, sticking the poster to the front window of the shop and raising her eyebrows at Mr Southcliffe who stood outside in the rain. He indicated with hand gestures and she reached forward again with another wobble to lift the top right corner a centimetre. She looked at him again. He smiled and gave her a thumbs up and she breathed a sigh of relief as she pressed the bottom two corners firmly. She hopped down from the chair as Mr Southcliffe re-entered the shop, the bell tinkling in her ear.

"That's fine Susan, thank you dear."

"No problem Mr Southcliffe."

"Oh I do hate halloween," he sighed as he walked back behind the counter. "All those silly pumpkins and ghosts."

"Oh but people love Halloween," she replied. "Just remember, everyone loves having parties. Parties mean photographs and that means we get more people in here wanting new cameras, frames and all the other stuff. Not everyone knows how to do stuff on their computers. It's worth the effort. We always make loads of profit at this time of year."

"It's not as if these silly posters are even frightening," he moaned. "Now if we could come up with something really frightening, that would be something worth putting in the window."

"What did you have in mind?" she asked, trying to sound interested in an effort to avoid having to spend the rest of the day listening to his moaning.

"Well, as you know I do a lot of reading about photography, and there's one book that's really got me thinking. In the early days you

1

know, people thought that photographs captured the person's soul and it took a long time before photography became accepted and trusted."

"Oh that's silly," she laughed.

"Possibly, but it led me to thinking about the essence of emotions and whether they could be captured on film," he began and Susan groaned inwardly as he then went on to lecture her about his interest in esoteric photography, whatever that was. She tried to look interested, nodded from time to time with a smile and let her mind wander to what she was going to wear to the halloween party her girlfriends had invited her to.

"So I thought you might like to help me," he finished and Susan snapped out of her musings.

"Help you? How?"

"By modelling for me so I can try it out."

"Try what out?"

"Oh Susan, weren't you listening?"

"Well yes I was but you lost me somewhere in the middle," she smiled, embarrassed.

"I've been tinkering with an old plate camera and come up with my own special photographic plates that I've treated in such a way so that when exposed in ultra violet light, they should capture the more subtle energies like those given off by our emotions."

"Oh, you mean like those aura cameras that people use at psychic fairs and stuff?"

"It's a similar principle yes, but I hope that mine is going to be more sensitive and pick up not only the body's natural energy field, but the very thoughts and emotions you're feeling when I take the photograph."

"So all I have to do is sit there and think about things?"

"Basically yes," he nodded. "I'll show you pictures, ask you questions and play music etc, to try to induce you to feel a particular emotion so that I can then try to photograph it."

"Well that sounds okay," she grinned. "For time and a half obviously."

"Susan, you're a sharp business woman," he grinned. "Just think what a scoop that would be to photograph the energy of joy, love, anger or fear. Not just photographs of people feigning those emotions, but the actual energy of the emotion itself. We'd be famous Susan, and rich. We could both retire early."

"Sounds wonderful. I'll make some coffee and get some choccy biccies to go with it. If we're going to be rich and famous, we can splash out on choccy biccies don't you think?"

"Indeed I do," he laughed.

The phone rang and Susan put down her magazine and picked it up. "Southcliffe and McGregor Photographic Supplies, how can I help?"

"Oh hi Sue it's Jeff here. How's your day going?"

"Hi Jeff, not bad thanks."

"Great. Look I'm really sorry but I can't make it tonight. The ex wants me to have Jack this evening so she can go off with her new beau, and I didn't like to refuse. Anything to encourage her into the arms of another fool so she'll stop hounding me for more money."

"That's okay, no worries. Mr Southcliffe wants me to help him try out some new fangled camera he's been tinkering with so you needn't feel guilty this time."

"Okay that's great. I'll ring you around eleven so you can kiss me goodnight."

"I'll look forward to it. Give Jack a kiss for me."

"Will do. Take care. I love you."

"Love you too." She put down the phone and sighed. At least she could get her promise to help Mr Southcliffe out of the way. He was delighted when she told him of her broken appointment that meant she was free that very evening if he wanted to play with his new toy. He positively beamed and rushed down to the basement to prepare everything and she didn't see him for the rest of the afternoon.

The last few customers finally left and Susan closed up and emptied her till. Once the takings were in the safe, she headed towards the back of the shop and called down to the basement.

"Mr Southcliffe? I've closed up so give me a shout when you need me."

"Anytime you like dear, come on down as they say." She sighed and started down the stairs into the gloom. It was dark down there and her eyes took a minute or two to adjust. She could hear Mr Southcliffe padding about in his slippers and she grinned. Why he always wore slippers down here she didn't know but it amused her.

"Ahh there you are," he said as he appeared to her right and made her jump. "Sorry it's dark but these plates I've been experimenting with need very low light. Let me just get them put into this new dark box I've made and I'll turn a light on." She waited as he padded off. She heard a click and then a low red bulb went on. "There we are, that's better," he smiled. "Now, all I need you to do is to sit down there and listen to what I say. I'm going to give you verbal cues that I hope will induce specific emotions within your brain so that I can then photograph them."

"Okay, that sounds easy enough," she smiled.

"How about changing into something a little more umm, atmospheric?" he suggested. She frowned and he laughed. "Oh come on now, don't look like that. You know very well I'm gay. Tut tut Susan, the very thought," he laughed and she blushed. "Let's see what I've got in this box of stuff. Ahh yes what about this?" he offered as he held up a beautiful victorian nightgown. "This will set the scene and maybe if you let your hair down and possibly even a bare shoulder to add a little risqué touch? There's a screen over there so you can change without worrying about me leering at you and I'll hum whilst I fiddle about here so you'll know I'm not creeping up on you."

It was a bit cramped behind the screen but Susan had to admit she thought the whole idea was rather fun, if a little silly, and if she got a nice photograph or two out of it to give to Jeff, then all well and good.

4

Delectus Morbidium

She put the nightgown on, let down her hair and ruffled it up a bit before stepping out and doing a twirl. Mr Southcliffe grinned from ear to ear and clapped his hands together at the sight of her.

"Oh you're perfect my dear, just perfect. Now just sit down, over there. Just close your eyes and listen to my voice. Now think about someone you love dearly. Think about holding them, kissing them and being close to them." A couple of flashes came to her through her closed eyelids and then some muttering.

"Now think of something that made you very angry. Think of that feeling and let yourself feel it again now." More flashes and muttering.

"Okay now think of something that frightens you." She could not help but think of spiders. She had hated them since childhood and just the thought of them terrified her. A couple more flashes and excited murmuring from Mr Southcliffe.

"Wonderful Susan. It seems fear is your strongest emotion and I'm not surprised given how terrified you are of spiders. Think of them crawling up your arm, sitting on the pillow next to you. You awake and see them out of the corner of your eyes and leap up, terrified out of your wits. Feel it Susan, really feel it."

She was feeling it all right. Her heart was pounding and she could feel beads of sweat beginning to break out on her forehead. She thought she heard Mr Southcliffe padding around in his slippers but she could not get the image of a huge spider on her pillow out of her mind and she cursed him. She knew she would be sleeping on the sofa tonight and it would be all his fault.

"See how they move Susan, it's horrible isn't it? The way they scuttle along like that, all legs going everywhere, it's terrifying isn't it?" Without warning, she felt her wrists and ankles suddenly bound tightly to the chair. She opened her eyes in terror to find Mr Southcliffe behind her. He laughed into her ear.

"You see Susan, I love to tinker with things and once I realised what I'd invented with this camera, I needed a volunteer to help me.

5

The problem is though, who is going to be willing to sit still whilst being terrified out of their wits hmm? So, I tinkered with this chair too and now you can wriggle and scream as much as you like. In fact, scream all you want; it'll just make you more frightened and help me even more."

Susan burst into tears and begged him to let her free. She wrestled with the bindings that held her firm but she could not free herself.

"I know what your greatest fear is Susan, don't I?" he coo'ed, "and your fear is going to make me very rich and very famous." He walked back to the camera and smiled at her as he picked up a small box and pressed a button on the top. She heard a whining noise from above and looked up to see something descending towards her in the gloom. Only when it was just a few inches above her head could she make out what it was and once she saw the perspex container filled with a writhing mass of spiders, she went cold through to the bone. Her eyes widened in shock as she looked from the box, to Mr Southcliffe and then back to the box again as she realised what he was about to do to her.

"No. Please no," she begged. "Anything but that please. I'll do anything. Please don't."

"Feel the fear Susan," he replied. "Really feel it."

The light went out and she heard a click. Time stood still as she waited for the inevitable. Less than two seconds later she felt herself being drenched in a sudden tidal wave that wriggled and squirmed. She felt scuttling and scurrying over her shoulders and down her neck as something settled onto her left eye. Her hair seemed alive, and when she realised why, she let out the first scream. Flashes hit her and in the flashes she saw them; some tiny and others, huge. Millions of them covered her and as she screamed, she felt something rush into her mouth and sit on her tongue.

She spat convulsively and then became aware of a sharp pain in her neck. She screamed and wriggled and the camera flashed as, in their hundreds, they bit her. She was vaguely aware of another whining noise above and she cried in terror. The light flashed on and she looked up just in time to see hundreds of huge tarantulas falling towards her. She screamed and screamed and as the bites began to take effect, she felt her body relaxing and when she could no longer scream, she waited for darkness to come.

THE END

ABDUCTION
starring Cody Martin & Tracey Gore

"But Cody doesn't believe me," Tracey wailed.

Hannah rolled her eyes and tried to suppress a grin. "I doubt many people would love."

"He says I'm either making it all up to cover up that I cheated on him or that I was high and hallucinating."

"Did you cheat on him?" Hannah looked at Tracey with raised eyebrows.

"Of course not. Whose side are you on?"

"I'm not taking sides. Come on, don't get defensive. You have to admit though, alien abduction? That's quite a stretch for anyone to believe. Listen, I'm sure he'll forgive you if you own up and say you're sorry."

"But I didn't cheat on him," Tracey wailed. "Everything I told him was the truth."

Hannah sighed deeply and forced herself to smile and tried to change the subject. She was worried for Tracey and secretly believed Cody. She knew her friend often smoked weed and she was not confident that she could be faithful to any man. When they were in high school together, Tracey had been a bit of a wild child and had the beginnings of a bad reputation by the time they left. Hannah was relieved when Tracey got a job at the local diner and met Cody. He was good for her and they seemed happy, but now this ridiculous alien abduction thing was threatening to break them up. Hannah knew she must avoid interfering but she felt torn between the two.

Cody picked at his pie and tried not to think about the fact that his girlfriend, the love of his life had probably cheated on him but try as he might, the thoughts raced around inside his head and almost drove him crazy. He wondered if he should end it with Tracey but dismissed that thought right away. He had loved her from the moment he first laid eyes on her and he knew there was no one else in this two-bit town to take her place at his side or in his bed. He thought back over the arguments they had over the past few weeks; the screaming and name calling, and he felt ashamed as he realised that he was driving her away. He could not imagine life without her so he made a decision that if she cheated on him then it was obviously his fault for not making her happy.

He looked up at her as she stared blankly down at her plate and sighed quietly.

"I'm sorry baby," he whispered. "Forgive me for not being there for you. Can we start over?"

"I didn't cheat on you Cody," she replied, "and it makes me sad and angry that you don't believe me."

"Then let's put all this behind us and move on. Draw a line in the sand and live our life as we always said we wanted to huh? We both said things when we were angry and I apologise for everything I said and did to make you sad. Can you forgive me and move on with me?"

The sex that night was easily the best since the day they first began dating. All the weeks of emotional stress drove them both to heights they had never experienced before. Tracey was insatiable; she was the perfect whore in bed and Cody was in heaven as she teased him with her mouth until he could feel his orgasm approaching. He began to moan and she sat astride him and let him watch her teasing her own clitoris as he thrust into her. Her insides convulsed and squeezed him to a bone crunching orgasm and they cried out together as the waves of euphoria overwhelmed them. Before the dawn broke, he had taken her in every way either of them could think of and both were surprised at the strength of their desires. The room stank of sex as they awoke and as Cody thrust into her from behind, the bed head thumping into the wall, their cries echoed around the house and even reached the ears of the raccoon that was busy stealing scraps from their trash-can. They could not get enough of each other. Tracey dropped to her knees as they showered together and suckled greedily as he exploded into her mouth.

Delectus Morbidium

Cody took her from behind as she washed the dishes at the kitchen sink. He took her up against the side wall of the barn, both naked as the day they were born and yelling at the tops of their voices as their orgasms overtook them. Cody thought back to when they first started dating and how shy she was when he made sexual advances towards her. She seemed a different woman now, ever since the day she said the aliens abducted her, ever since the day he reckoned she cheated on him.

"Are you sure Doc?" Cody asked with a grin.

"Oh yes, quite sure. Congratulations both of you."

"When is it due?" Tracey asked with tears in her eyes.

"I estimate that he or she should arrive around about the second week of March, give or take."

"That's awesome," Cody replied with tears on his cheeks. "Hey honey we're gonna have a baby. A real family huh?"

"I can't believe it," she replied with a smile. "I never thought I'd be having a family like nice folks do. We'll do it right won't we Cody?"

"We'll be the best parents ever," he said as he squeezed her hand and kissed her.

"Now," the doctor interrupted, "I'll arrange for all your ante natal care, scans etc and all of the usual rigmarole so don't worry. You'll get a letter within a couple of weeks with a date for a scan and I want you to visit me again a week after that. Now go and look forward to being parents. Make sure you eat well, plenty of fresh fruit and vegetables and lean meat and fish. Not too much alcohol mind, but a glass or two a week won't hurt. You already gave up smoking so that's not an issue. If your morning sickness gets too bad, come back and see me and I'll give you something to ease it. Any time you're worried you can call the duty nurse."

Tracey's bump got big and Cody was proud. When the time came for them to have their first scan, they were like excited kids on Christmas morning. The nurse helped Tracey up onto the bed and got her comfortable before spreading some icy cold goo all over her bump and switching on the scanner. A sudden sharp pain stabbed through

11

Tracey's abdomen and she winced and clasped a hand to her side. A loud pop made them all jump and the scanner went dead and no amount of fiddling by the nurse could get it to work again, so they went home disappointed and waited for another appointment. When the second appointment arrived, Tracey woke up that morning covered from head to foot in red spots which defied all efforts by the visiting doctor to correctly diagnose. When the third appointment arrived, Cody's car stalled and refused to be started and they both began to worry that they would never be able to get a scan done.

The midwife visited regularly and everything went smoothly until Tracey's due date came, and went. The kindly midwife assured them that the baby was healthy and that in her opinion, the doctor got the dates wrong as her experienced hands told her the little mite had a few weeks to go yet. They both watched videos of babies being born and what to do if he or she decides to arrive before the midwife could travel the ten miles or so to their house. Meanwhile Cody painted the nursery in a genderless shade of sunny yellow and put together the same cot his own parents had used when he was born. Tracey was long since passed able to enjoy sex with Cody in their usually active way, so she made sure to give him as much pleasure as she could with her hands and occasionally she let him pleasure himself into her mouth. She missed the sex they shared before she got so big but Cody took care to give her pleasure with his tongue and his expert fingers. It was as they were both reaching orgasm together one night in early April that it began. Tracey was sucking hard on Cody's swollen cock and massaging his shaft as he flicked her clitoris with his tongue and she felt the warmth flood over her tongue as her own body shuddered. Their shared orgasm was just beginning to wane as the first pain gripped her, making her cry out in shock at the severity of it.

Cody raced to the telephone and called the midwife who told him not to worry and that she would be with him within a half hour, before racing back up as she screamed the house down. He held her hand, kissed her cheek and mopped her brow as she screamed as the minutes ticked by and the midwife still did not arrive. Suddenly a great rush of liquid came from Tracey's crotch and soaked the bed and Cody realised that he might just be on his own here. He forced his mind back to the videos they had watched and the advice they had been given in the event of an emergency. Tracey screamed again but this time gave an involuntary push and raised her knees.

"No baby, don't push honey."

"I can't help it," she hissed. "I just have to."

With another enormous push, Cody and Tracey's life crashed down around their ears and within twenty minutes it was all over. The infant slid out onto the bed between Tracey's thighs and lay their mewling; its dark grey, waxy skin glistening from the liquid it had lived within for the past ten months. Its huge oval black eyes blinked at the sudden light and its tail whipped as it cried and Cody's jaw dropped in shock as he looked at it.

"What is it?" Tracey gasped. "Boy or girl?"

Cody looked and frowned as he tried to make sense of what he saw. It was clearly a boy; it's large, semi erect penis told him that right away. Thinking back to the videos they both watched while Tracey's bump grew, he could not remember any of the newborns looking like this. His next thought was to remember Tracey's story, all those months back, and how easily he had assumed she was lying to cover up cheating on him. All at once he felt sorry to have mistrusted her and yet, still his mind could not accept what his eyes were seeing. Like most folks, Cody had seen movies about aliens abducting unsuspecting victims from their beds and doing experiments on them, but no one really believes that shit really happens, not here. He wondered how many other women were carrying such creatures within their wombs; was this the first wave of an invasion?

The midwife drove her elderly car at a reckless pace up the country road that led to Tracey and Cody's farm. She had found herself stuck behind an accident involving two huge trucks and a car with no way of getting around them and had to sit and wait for over an hour. She turned into the driveway, headed for the barn and sighed with relief at having got there at last. She hoped everything was okay and tried to calm herself as she approached the back door. The first shot rang out and rooted her to the spot. The second made her almost jump out of her skin and the third made her cry out in shock. She reached for the door handle and realised that she was probably not going to be delivering a baby this evening.

THE END

AUNTY
starring Lesley Hazelhurst & Rebecca Brockman

Lesley put down the newspaper and drained the last of her rapidly cooling tea. It was a beautiful summer afternoon and the garden looked lovely.

"Oh isn't this just wonderful?" Aunt Rebecca sighed as she settled back in her lounger. "The perfect afternoon, on a perfect summer's day. I wish it could stay like this moment forever."

"So do I," Lesley nodded, "but that's impossible unfortunately. You know Aunty, we're going to have to move soon."

"Move?" Aunt Rebecca looked up and slid her sunglasses down her nose to peer at her niece. "Why ever would we want to do that?"

"We can't afford to keep this place going for too much longer. Uncle Jim's money has nearly gone, you're retired and I can't afford to run this place on a secretary's pay."

"Oh don't you worry dear. Something will turn up, you'll see."

"Something like what?" Lesley laughed. "A miracle perhaps?"

"Maybe. Or perhaps a new rich uncle."

"What?" Lesley sat bolt upright in her chair and looked at her Aunt. "You've got yourself a new boyfriend? No, really?"

Aunt Rebecca grinned at Lesley and winked.

"Well?" Lesley demanded.

"Well what?" Aunt Rebecca replied.

"Who is he and what's he like?"

"His name is Bob Hatterwaite and he's a retired policeman. A chief inspector no less."

"I should think so," Lesley laughed. "I wouldn't want my Aunt hobnobbing with constables now would I?"

Both women laughed out loud and spent the rest of the afternoon gossiping about him and making plans for Aunt Rebecca's new romance, how they planned to enjoy his extremely healthy pension and income from his stocks and shares.

For a woman of Aunt Rebecca's age, the romance was of such a whirlwind nature that it would have been regarded as scandalous when she was a young woman. By the first snowfall they were married and enjoying a three week cruise for their honeymoon whilst Lesley had the large rambling home to herself so long as she obeyed her Aunt's strict instructions as to the daily care of her beloved plants. Lesley was not into plants but she knew her Aunt's were pretty special, so she made the effort to look after them as per instructions, and when the newlyweds returned home, Rebecca was delighted to see her babies were in good health.

Bob was more than happy for Lesley to continue living in the East wing of the large house. It enabled her to carry on looking after her aunt so he did not have to give up his golf or fishing with his ex-police buddies. Rebecca was a good wife, he decided. She fed him well and did everything for him and even the sex was good, for a woman of her age. He could take her to official functions without being embarrassed, she never got drunk and he did not have to worry about her having an affair with a younger man. It also meant he was still free to enjoy the occasional liaison with his favourite young prostitute without his new wife having to be horrified at his lewd suggestions as to what he would like her to do to him. His grown up children from his previous marriage were happy with Rebecca and loved coming to stay for the weekend with the grandchildren. The large house was set in three acres of its own land and the nearest neighbour was a mile away. Built in the middle of green belt land in the Home Counties, there was no need to worry about waking up to find a housing estate next door.

It was during the spring, while the house was being rewired to bring it up to modern standards that Bob started to feel ill. Just a slight chest pain at first, it quickly escalated into a full blown heart attack and Bob was rushed to hospital, leaving Lesley to oversee the workmen who had by now finished the rewiring and been replaced by builders putting up a new conservatory. He was soon home to convalesce and enjoyed being fussed over by Rebecca whilst watching the new double glazing go in, the new central heating system being fitted and the whole house being redecorated. By the time the new carpets had been laid, he was up and about again and back to his old self and enjoying his twice weekly golf and prostitute.

Things came to a head in late spring, when Rebecca and Lesley went to the BotGene convention in central London. During her working years, Rebecca, or Doctor Rebecca Brockman as she was known in those days, was an expert in plant genetics and specialised in medicinal plants. She was responsible for genetically engineering several innocent looking garden flowers into repositories of powerful medicines that were now routinely used in hospitals all around the western world. She still enjoyed keeping in touch with her old colleagues at the conventions and liked to keep up to date with the latest discoveries and advancements in the field. Lesley decided to tag along with her and go shopping in Bond Street while her aunt nattered with her crusty old friends.

They had only been at the place forty minutes when there was a terrorist alert and everyone had to evacuate the building. After a further hour and a half, the police announced they were closing off the entire area for at least the next twenty four hours. After a couple of hours shopping, the two ladies went home hours earlier than planned, only to discover Bob right in the middle of the back lawn, trousers bagged around his ankles and penis buried deep inside the backside of a young blonde who couldn't have been more than twenty five. What made it worse was that the young blonde was a man, dressed as a guardsman, complete with bearskin, which had, due to the frantic nature of the men's coupling, started rapidly falling down over his face.

Rebecca, all sixty eight years of her, didn't rush forward yelling and screaming as any other woman might. Instead, she peered from around the corner of the house and instructed Lesley to retrieve her camera from her capacious handbag. Setting the state of the art device to video mode, she spent the next eighteen minutes recording her husband's dalliance and when, with a loud grunt from Bob, it was all over, she calmly packed the camera away, got back into her car with Lesley and drove to the nearest town for afternoon tea and cakes.

Bob was easily persuaded to hand over the entirety of his bank account to his new wife, along with his secret, up to now, life savings he'd put away in a building society. He sold his father's home in the north of Scotland he had been left after the old man died and gave the money to Rebecca with a smile. When he began to suffer with severe migraines, he had to give up golf and sold his top of the range clubs, with Rebecca's blessing of course and she nursed him herself right up until he died four months later of an aneurysm. The funeral was something of an occasion, with all of Bob's ex-police buddies in attendance, his golfing friends, his children and grandchildren and even several ex-cons he had put behind bars.

The following spring, Lesley and Rebecca were once again enjoying tea on the patio in the warm afternoon.

"I got a letter from the bank manager today," Rebecca announced. "All the official stuff is finally over and even after the children and grandchildren have their cut, we've enough to live comfortably at least until I die."

"Which ones was it then?" Lesley grinned and Rebecca giggled.

"Well the latin name," Rebecca began but Lesley cut her off.

"Oh come on, you know I'm hopeless with those long names."

"The ones with the small purple flowers, by the old butler's sink."

"Flowers, leaves or roots?"

"Flowers for headaches, roots for the aneurysm. Dried and steeped in boiling water and added to hot strong tea."

"You're a genius Aunty," Lesley laughed and Rebecca grinned.

"Not bad for a year's work eh?"

"Not bad at all."

"You know Lesley, we have enough to live comfortably but there's always room for improvement. You were on about that sports car the other day."

"The Porsche?"

"That's the one. If you want one of those, and maybe a swimming pool in the garden, or if I fancied that big emerald necklace we saw in London the other week, we need a new plan."

"What do you have in mind?"

"Maybe it's time you found Mr Right."

"The two women laughed loudly, their laughter carried off by the light spring breeze.

THE END

Merita King

BIG BROTHER

starring Rob Leggett, Donna Spencer & Brian Bigelow

Donna pouted as her mother donned her coat and headed towards the door. She was horror stricken when she had calmly announced over breakfast that she must spend the day with Rob while she went to visit Gran in hospital. The news had put her right off her chocolate flakes and despite pleading and slamming her fist on the table, her protestations had fallen on deaf ears.

Donna hated her older brother. He had bullied her for as long as she could remember and never failed to make fun of her whenever he had his silly friends round. He called her 'the runt' or 'the brat' and always made her cry and then laughed at her. Donna couldn't understand why he seemed to enjoy embarrassing her in front of his stupid spotty mates, who looked liked they never washed and leered at her all the time. He was only two years older than her, but she often felt him to be much younger than his fifteen years; sometimes he acted like a ten year old. A couple of the boys he hung out with were older than both of them, and one of them was not bad looking. If he was not a mate of Rob's she might consider dating him. Brian Bigelow had a car so he was a popular boy in their town and Rob always tried to emulate him, much to Donna's amusement.

She heard the car cough into life and watched out the window as her mother pulled out of the drive and headed off towards town. She sighed inwardly and hoped Rob would not be quite so horrible today. The sound of his chair scraping across the tiled floor brought her back from her musings and she turned to see him grab his mobile phone and head into the garden. Her heart sank for she knew this meant he was phoning his mates who would be here within minutes and making themselves thoroughly at home. She wished she had a lock on her bedroom door and made a vow to save her pocket money to buy one.

"Remember mum said to rake those leaves," she reminded him when he returned from the garden, mobile phone in hand.

"Oh shut up runt," he glowered at her.

"Well if you don't do it I'll tell her you had all your stupid mates over here all day looking through her things," she threatened.

"You wouldn't dare," he hissed as he turned to face her, his face like thunder.

He was right, but she threatened anyway. "Oh yeah? Just you wait."

"If you do that then I'll tell Brian you fancy him," he sniggered.

She reddened, her mouth open in shock. "Don't you dare you moron."

"So shut the fuck up then." He stuck out his chin to push his point home and flounced out of the kitchen.

The unmistakeable sound of Brian's car reached her ears and almost without thinking, she ran her hands through her hair and smoothed the front of her blouse. Voices reached her ears as the engine stopped and she heard an unfamiliar female voice amongst them. Her hopes lifted a little. Maybe another girl around would make Rob and his friends' company a little more bearable. She turned and the ready smile fell from her lips as she watched Brian enter their kitchen arm in arm with Jeena, the pretty blonde girl from three streets away.

Brian looked at Donna and grinned. "Hey runt," he sneered and Jeena giggled as she snuggled into his chest. Donna turned away, not wanting anyone to see her burning cheeks but Rob had seen.

"What's up runt?" he asked with a snigger, "why are you blushing huh?" Several more sniggers reached Donna's ears and she forced herself not to cry as she busied herself with washing up the breakfast dishes. Rob was not going to let it lie though and he continued his taunting. "Maybe she's jealous huh? Jealous of Jeena perhaps?" Guffaws of laughter echoed around the kitchen and something inside Donna snapped.

She spun around and glared at Rob. "No you moron," she spat, "I'm not jealous at all. I feel sorry for the stupid cow." The laughter died and the kitchen went eerily silent. She glared at Rob for a few moments before stamping outside to rake the leaves as her mother had asked. She knew he was not going to do it, and although she hated the thought of saving his ass, it gave her the opportunity to get away from them for a while and, if she was careful, she could spin the job out and make it last at least an hour.

The wind was chilly up here near the cliffs but Donna did not mind; she loved the view out to sea and was very happy that the end of their large garden was just fifty yards from the cliff edge, with only the cliff path between their weathered wooden fencing and the vastness of the ocean. Seagulls screeched overhead as she raked the fallen leaves from the Oak and Ash trees that screened them from their next door neighbour's garden. She managed to make the job last just over an hour and by the time she finished she was hot and worn out. She looked at the large pile of leaves by the gap in the fence and sighed as she went to fetch the garden rubbish bag.

"Donna?" The voice almost startled her out of her wits and she spun around to see Jeena standing behind her. "What did you mean you feel sorry for me?"

Donna grinned. She was happy that the silly cow had fallen for it. "Well it's not my place to say really," she replied and turned away to the leaf pile, knowing Jeena would follow and grinning to herself when she heard her footsteps behind.

"Oh come on Donna," Jeena coaxed. "If you know something, you have to tell me."

Donna padded softly into the hall to fetch her coat, hoping she would not be heard. She crept out, ran across the back garden and slipped through the gap in the fence to stand on the cliff path. A liner slid effortlessly across the horizon and she wondered where it was going and wished that wherever it was, she was going too. She smiled as she imagined herself standing on deck, gown flowing in the breeze as the music played softly in the background.

"Where's Jeena?" a voice behind her said and her dreams vanished away. She turned and looked into Brian's fairly handsome face. "Well? Where is she runt?"

"Why do you call me that?" she asked sadly. "My name is Donna, not runt."

Brian sighed and rolled his eyes. "Okay okay. Donna, where is Jeena?"

"She went home," she replied.

"Home?" he frowned. "Why?"

"She went off in a huff when I told her I knew what was going on between her and Rob," she said flatly and waited for him to react.

His eyebrows shot to the top of his spotty forehead. "What?"

"You heard," she replied and went to turn away.

"She's been carrying on with your brother? No way. You're making that up."

"If you say so," she sighed.

"If this is some kind of joke than you'd better say so now because I'm going to bust his head in if it's true," he said as he grabbed her arm and turned her to face him.

"Maybe you should bust her head in too," she said. "She's the one that's cheated on you. Rob's just a spotty moron without a girlfriend of his own; who can blame him if she threw herself at him." She watched as he turned and marched back to the house and out of sight and grinned as she waited for something to happen. She did not have to wait long and laughed out loud as shouts could be heard and then a yell of pain. Brian suddenly reappeared around the side of the garden, marching towards his car with the other two spotty lads. The car coughed into life on the fourth attempt and she watched it slide out into the lane and roar off into the distance, the angry gear changing reaching her ears for almost a minute before the screeching of the seagulls took over.

Donna wondered how Rob would react and decided it would be best to let him stew for a while before going back inside, so she headed over to the bag of leaves and dragged it towards the cliff edge so she could tip it over and let the wind and sea take care of them. The slamming of the door made her spin around to see Rob marching up the garden towards her, blood trickling from the corner of his mouth and one eye already beginning to swell shut. Inwardly she grinned but she managed to feign concern.

"What happened to you?" she asked.

"You fucking little brat," he spat at her. "You're gonna pay for that, runt."

"For what?" she asked, trying to sound perplexed.

"You told Brian I was seeing Jeena, didn't you?"

"What? Don't be daft you moron. Is that how you earned that black eye then?"

"How could you do that? Why?" he yelled.

"Why not?" she yelled back. "That's what a runt does isn't it? Typical runt behaviour huh? Besides, you've written about her in your diary. I've read it all. You're sick, a pervert that's what you are. The next time you call me runt I'll show Brian and all your other stupid spotty mates too. I've got photos of it all on my mobile phone and on my facebook."

"What?" Rob yelled as he went white. "You've put them on facebook? Oh fuck Donna what did you have to do that for?"

"Relax moron, they're set so only I can see them. For now anyway. Remember that the next time you call me runt or be rude to me with your stupid mates okay? Now help me get these leaves tipped over the cliff, mum will be home soon and I've already done your job for you. You owe me half your pocket money for that."

Rob sighed heavily as he stooped to the big garden bag that was full of leaves. He heaved it over to the cliff and bent to tip them over the edge.

Donna winced as she heard the crunch but smiled inwardly. She knew mum would be heartbroken of course, just as she was when dad took an overdose of sleeping tablets but she would get over it. He had been a bully too and it was him who had given her the nickname runt.

She was delighted to discover her mother's sleeping tablets when she made the beds that morning. She supposed Jeena's mother would be heartbroken too but, like her mother, she would get over it.

THE END

BOUNDARIES
starring Sheryl Galzote & Tracey Tabor

Tracey smiled and thanked the woman at the checkout. After gathering her purchases, she exited the small delicatessen and delighted at the tinkling of the little bell on the door. This must be a local tradition, she thought to herself as she turned left and strolled along, gazing into shop windows. It seemed as though every single shop in this town had those little bells on their doors and the soft tinkling they made sounded like fairy music to her ears. She had come to Allensville after her divorce, which happened to coincide with her favourite aunt dying and leaving her a large house in two acres of garden at the edge of this small backwater town. The sale of the marital home had not yielded enough for her to buy another place in the city, so she cut her losses and moved out here to start over. Several of the local shops were happy to take in her craftwork to sell and the town was not so far away that she could not still commute back into the city to help run the successful craft store she owned. She had to take on a couple of new staff members which would enable her to work just three days a week instead of the usual six but her business partner Andrew encouraged her, saying she was burning herself out with such a workload. They both worked two different days each week and shared Saturdays so they could discuss any problems, make plans for the future of the business and check over the books.

Tracey found out quickly that Allensville was a religious community and within the first forty-eight hours of taking over possession of her aunt's house, three different local people informed her that she would be expected to attend services at the local church. She did not mind, she was brought up in a family that went to church regularly and although she would never call herself devout, she believed in some kind of creator. Besides, she realised, it would be an ideal opportunity to make friends and maybe even extend her sales network a little. The Church of Desegregation nestled within the boundary of the Galzote family farm in a purpose built wooden building, built by local people who had donated the materials, their expertise and their time. The outside was painted white with a frieze around the top with painted symbols that Tracey did not recognise. One thing that surprised her was the total lack of the usual religious symbols she might expect to see in a church. There was no cross, crucifix or angels, no holy water, no paintings of the last supper, no statues of Mary gazing benevolently down upon the parishioners. The inside walls were as white as the outside and the same frieze adorned all four walls.

"It's lovely to see you here Miss umm?" The voice made Tracey jump and she turned to see a woman smiling.

"Tabor," she replied with a smile. "Tracey Tabor. I've just recently moved to Allensville and several people invited me to attend services here, so here I am."

"You're very welcome," the woman replied. "I am Sheryl Galzote, Minister of the Church of Desegregation."

They shook hands and Tracey ventured to ask about the obvious lack of religious icons and paraphernalia in the church.

Sheryl smiled. "We don't worship God or Jesus here Tracey. We are not here to believe blindly in dogma handed down but unproven for thousands of years. We are the Church of Desegregation and that is what we strive to achieve. The bringing down of all the boundaries that separate one man from another, one being from another. We aim to become a race without boundaries of race, creed or belief and all of the rules and regulations man imposes upon himself that limit our ability to truly integrate with all of creation are what we fight against."

"I'm not sure I totally understand," Tracey replied.

"It does seem complicated at first," Sheryl nodded. "Don't worry though; you'll come to understand in time."

"Are you saying you don't have rules in Allensville?" Tracey asked.

"Sheryl laughed out loud. "No of course not. Our children still go to school, we still pay our bills and we will prosecute you if you steal from us. We have all the usual social rules to ensure our society runs smoothly, just as all societies do, but we don't have any rules or beliefs that further segregate one being from another."

"Like racism," Tracey offered.

"Yes, that's a perfect example. We do not allow anything that shows a belief in, or adherence to, anything that would promote the belief that one race is lesser than another. In fact we promote social integration across racial boundaries and you may have noticed many couples in Allensville of different racial heritage."

Tracey had not really noticed but she nodded anyway.

"It is the same with different age groups," Sheryl continued. "We actively encourage the old and the young to integrate with each other, we encourage children of both sexes to play together and you will notice that our young children are dressed in ways that don't bring attention to their gender. Many people here of all ages prefer to dress in this fashion."

Tracey had noticed that and it had amused her when she had seen an old man walking down the street in what looked to her like a toga. "Yes I have noticed that," she nodded.

"We are constantly challenging all barriers to full integration and our discussion evenings are often quite interesting events. We can be discussing whether to stop segregating our children's classrooms by age and ability one minute and debating the merits of the accepted boundaries of good and evil the next."

"Good and evil?" Tracy asked. "You mean you even challenge that?"

"Yes of course we do. Only by debating and challenging society's accepted norms, can we hope to find more healthy ones for ourselves. Just because something has been a certain way for hundreds of years, does not make it necessarily right. You must join us; they're every Wednesday evening at seven thirty."

And so, Tracey became an active member of the Church of Desegregation. She sang their happy songs of unity and love for all

29

creation; she helped at bake sales and joined in the discussion evenings with fervour. One particularly lively debate was about angels and demons and whether the accepted views on them are warranted or whether the segregation is unjustified. One side argued that angels and demons could never be put under the same umbrella as one works for man's best interest whilst the other works for his own. The other side reminded them that even the devil was first created an angel and that angels have fought many wars, disobeyed God by fornicating with human women and that their power to smite people on a whim, is legendary.

"Why is it that we welcome angels into our company when they are historically known to commit acts of violence and yet we want demons to stay away?" Sheryl asked. "Why should we not welcome these beings as we do their brothers? Were they not born of the same father after all? Do we love our naughty children any less than those that behave well?" The debate continued for three hours and Tracey had to admit, she had never thought of it in detail before and although it pained her to admit it, Sheryl had a point. When she got home, she made herself some coffee and set about finishing the paintwork on her latest batch of crafts for her shop.

The following Saturday she arrived at the shop early and entered her new batch of crafts into the inventory, priced them up and had them on sale before Andrew arrived with hot coffee and croissants. It was the middle of the tourist season, the shop was busy, and business was brisk. Just after lunch, Tracey noticed an elderly man browsing the shelves and studying many items quite closely. Eventually he approached Tracey with a painted plant pot in his hand and asked her about the design she had painted around the top and bottom edges. She had copied the frieze from the church and used the many symbols in a lot of her latest batch of crafts.

"Excuse me Madam but where did you get the idea for these symbols as decoration for such everyday items?"

Delectus Morbidium

"Oh, they're from my local church. Those symbols, and many others, are painted on a frieze around the outside and on the inside too. They caught my eye so I copied some of them."

"A church you say? Oh no that can't be correct at all, you must be mistaken my dear."

"Mistaken? I assure you I am not mistaken. I sit in that church twice a week."

"Oh dear. That is not good. Not good at all," the man became agitated and Tracey looked at Andrew, who shrugged. "Oh dear me."

"Whatever is the matter?" she asked.

"Are you aware of the meaning of these symbols? If you are then all well and good, I suppose. After all, each to his own as they say, and who am I to condemn anyone's beliefs but if you do not know what they mean, then my dear. Then maybe you should learn."

"I've no idea what they mean," she replied. "I did ask the minister but she said they're just artwork. Do they have a meaning then?"

"Oh yes, indeed they do my dear. A very important meaning and one that you should be aware of, especially when using them to decorate your home. I'm a Professor of Ancient Languages at the University and I specialise in the Enochian language and its derivations."

"Enochian?" Andrew asked. "I've never heard of that."

"It's known as the ancient language of the angels," the Professor explained. "The language that the angels, and God allegedly, used in heaven. God sent some of his angels out to communicate with prophets and the language they used in those communications was, apparently, Enochian. It was also the language that Adam used in the Garden of Eden until his fall from grace and banishment, when he lost the use of it and formed his own language. That is one of the accepted histories of it anyway.

"Well it makes sense that it would be used to decorate a church then wouldn't it?" Tracey remarked and Andrew nodded.

"Indeed it would," the Professor nodded. "The trouble is not that it's Enochian. The trouble is what it's saying, the message it's giving. Tell me my dear, if you don't mind, what is your church called?"

31

"The Church of Desegregation," Tracey replied.

"And is it a Christian establishment?"

"Well I umm," Tracey thought about the lack of the usual iconography she would expect and was not sure of her answer. "Actually I'm not sure. I did think that was odd when I first went there. You see there are no crosses or crucifixes, no Mary or Jesus, angels or holy water. In fact, there is no holy anything that I can see. Even the songs we sing do not mention God, Jesus, Mary or any of the usual stuff you would expect. I've always assumed it was one of those modern life churches y'know?"

"Well I would urge you most strongly to stop attending at once," the Professor continued.

"Whatever for? Besides I have my full integration ceremony tomorrow."

"Oh dear me no," the Professor wrung his hands and bit his lower lip in anguish. "No you mustn't, you mustn't. Stay away from there altogether."

"So what do these symbols mean?" Andrew asked, intrigued now and wished the old guy would just get on with it and stop mumbling about doom and gloom.

"They are an invitation."

"An invitation?" Tracey exclaimed. "An invitation to what?"

"An invitation into the light of your soul. From what I can make out from the pieces you have on display, it is an invitation to something that normally dwells in darkness, to come and share the light of your soul."

"What sort of thing?" Andrew asked.

"I've no idea without seeing the whole frieze," the Professor replied, "but I urge you my dear, never to attend that place ever again. Please, just stay away." He put down the flowerpot and walked out, still mumbling to himself about staying away. Tracey looked at Andrew, who stared back in disbelief and then both burst out laughing.

The following evening, Tracey was ready for her full integration ceremony into the Church of Desegregation and it seemed as if the whole town was there to share it with her. She wore a simple shift and no underwear, as instructed by Sheryl. When Tracey had asked why she could not wear underclothes, Sheryl explained that for this symbolic ceremony there were to be no barriers between herself and the whole of creation. She sat at the front of the congregation during the songs, when they sang of unity with all creation and sharing the light of their souls with all beings. Once the singing was over, Sheryl approached Tracey.

"Why are you here amongst us?" She boomed.

"I wish for full integration," she replied, as Sheryl had instructed.

"Do you freely share the light of your soul with all beings in creation?"

"I do."

"Even those who, by order of those in fear, greed and envy, have been forced to dwell in the darkness of segregation from their brothers?"

"I do."

"Do you share the light of your soul freely?"

"I do."

"Then come. Stand upon the joining stone." Sheryl took Tracey's hand, led her up the three steps to a platform, raised a few inches above the floor, and bade her stand upon it. Tracey saw a hole in the centre and two painted footprints, one on either side. She placed her feet on the painted footprints and faced the congregation who all stood with arms raised and read from the frieze upon the walls.

"We call upon our brother in darkness to come and share this new light freely given by this enlightened soul. We invite you now, lost brother, to leave the pit and join with this woman who shares her light with you. We open the door for you and welcome you into our house. No longer shall you be consigned to hell dear brother, for now the kingdom of Earth is open to you. From darkness into light, from hell unto the Earth, from the depths into this woman."

Sheryl turned from the congregation and looked Tracey in the eyes as they chanted the last line, repeatedly. As Tracey gazed back into

Sheryl's eyes, she felt heat radiating up from below and looked down into the hole between her feet, which now glowed red, as if fire were reaching up to her. She tried to step away but her body would not move no matter how she tried. She was terrified and glanced at Sheryl, begging for help, begging her to stop but noticed the woman's eyes begin to glow red like the pit between her feet.

The chanting continued and Tracey screamed but Sheryl held her firm by some unseen force of mind. Her eyes now bright red and glowing, as were those of the whole congregation by now. The heat radiating up from the hole between her feet was now painful and Tracey looked down to see flames licking up from below, the glowing hot tunnel going down for miles into the Earth. A rumbling came up through her feet, faint at first but gradually increasing in intensity until the whole building was vibrating.

Tracey continued begging for help but Sheryl and the congregation continued their chanting.

"From darkness into light, from hell unto the Earth, from the depths into this woman."

One last look down at the fiery hole and Tracey saw a black mist rising up amidst the flames towards her. Abruptly the chanting stopped as the mist licked over the edge of the hole and rose towards Tracey's crotch. She was terrified and tried to wriggle herself free but she was unable to make any part of her body move. At first, she felt nothing from below and the shift she wore did not allow her to see what might be going on. Then she felt something touch her sexually, like a gentle finger stroking her and she cried out in shock and fear. The finger continued stroking her clitoris and then another finger entered her and gently thrusted in and out. Despite her fear, Tracey's body quickly responded and she soon closed her eyes and began to moan in pleasure. The finger thrusting into her began to swell to the size of a large penis and she felt invisible hands clasping her buttocks, dragging her in with each thrust. Tracey had never taken such a large penis inside of her before but this was more pleasure than she could ever have imagined.

As her body began to convulse, she cried out in ecstasy and with one last thrust, the black mist entered up throughout her body and took control.

Tracey was forced back into the furthest reaches of her mind by the strength of the demon possessing her. He was an immensely strong being and she stood no hope of regaining control, even if she had wanted to. That was the funny thing, she did not want to resist any more. The sheer strength and power coursing through her being was unlike anything she could have imagined. The sexual pleasure too, was immense; having this uninhibited being living inside her body was the most erotic thing she had ever experienced and she had only to think of them sharing her body for the most intense orgasm to quickly envelope her.

"Welcome My Lord Satan," the being that shared Sheryl's body said.

THE END

DINNER DATE

starring Rebecca Brown, Beverlee Ruhland & Emma Raby

Rebecca Brown shrugged off her overcoat and slipped out of her shoes. It was cold in town and she wished she had worn a scarf to protect her ears. She flung the pile of junk mail onto the hall stand and went straight to the kitchen to make coffee. Just as she was raising the cup to her lips, the phone rang. She sighed and put the cup down.

"Hello?"

"Hi Beck, it's only me."

"Oh hi Beverlee," she trilled while groaning inwardly. Much as Rebecca enjoyed her friend's company, Beverlee could talk the hind leg off a donkey and with hot coffee and an equally hot shower beckoning, she was not in the mood for a long gossip.

"I've got tickets to Hank's new movie tonight. Want to come with Emma and me?"

This news lifted Rebecca's spirits and she smiled. She had been a fan of Hank Derran for ages and had met Beverlee and Emma through a fan page on a social networking site. His latest movie was proving to be a box office smash as usual, and tonight was its first showing in their hometown.

"I'd love to," she grinned.

"Great," Beverlee replied. "Emma's picking me up at six, so we'll be round to you at twenty past. Time for a drink before the action eh?"

"Absolutely. I thought the movie was sold out for the whole week, how did you get three tickets?"

"A guy at work bought them for his wife to take two of her girlfriends for her birthday, but she dumped him yesterday so he sold them to me."

"That's great, for us I mean, not him," Rebecca said. "Are they good seats?"

"Halfway back, just left of centre."

"Awesome, not at all bad. We struck gold. How much do you want for my share?"

"Seven pounds fifty each."

"Okay, that's fine. I'll see you later then, better go have a shower."

"See you later, bye."

It was freezing queuing outside the cinema but the girls made friends with several other fans and spent the time chatting about Hank, how gorgeous he was, what they would like to do with him if they ever met him, and which of his movies were their favourites. They did not mind that he always played the same character, a gun toting guy who stumbles upon some trouble and eventually saves the day and gets the girl. To them, he could do no wrong and they loved him.

When they finally reached the front of the queue, the reason for the delay became apparent.

"Good evening ladies," the pretty blonde smiled. "Would you like to enter our competition to meet Hank Derran for dinner and a photo-shoot? The lucky winner and two friends will be driven to London in a stretched limo and be put up in a five star hotel for two nights. The first night you will meet Hank for dinner and a show. On the following afternoon, you will all be taken for an exclusive magazine photo-shoot with Hank and you will all receive a complimentary framed photograph of your choice, signed by Hank of course. You will all get a free makeover and the services of a top stylist and designer clothes for the shoot."

"Oh wow, yes we'd love to," Emma exclaimed as Rebecca and Beverlee nodded.

"Okay, just fill in your names, addresses and email on this form and put it into the box over there. The winner will be picked at random by the Manager once the movie is underway and a notice will be posted here announcing the name so remember to check the board on your way out. Good luck."

The lights dimmed and the chatter died away as the curtain opened. Two hours later the three were grinning from ear to ear as the credits rolled.

"Wow, that's his best movie yet," Emma gasped.

"Oh my god he's more gorgeous than ever," Beverlee sighed.

"I'm definitely buying it on dvd when it comes out," Rebecca said. "I can't have a gap in my Derran collection now can I?"

"Of course not," Emma grinned.

"Perish the thought," Beverlee laughed.

"Shall we get a take away and head back to mine?" Rebecca offered and the other two nodded. They let the crowd thin down a bit before rising from their seats to leave and slowly making their way back towards the main entrance. "Indian or Chinese?" Rebecca asked.

Before the others could answer, they all heard several people murmuring Rebecca's name.

"Oh it's someone called Rebecca Brown," pouted a busty blonde to their left.

"Probably some fat old hag," replied her redheaded friend and they both laughed.

"What the fuck?" Emma said as she wheeled around.

"I'll give her fat old hag," Rebecca snorted as she made to follow them out. Before she had taken a step she felt someone tugging at her coat.

"Hey Beck," Beverlee gasped. "Look Hun."

"What?

"Look."

"Look at what?"

"Look at that," Beverlee commanded. Rebecca and Emma followed her pointing finger and gazed up at the poster advertising the movie they had just seen. Across the middle of the poster, in giant red letters, was an announcement from the manager.

'The winner of the Meet Hank Derran for Dinner competition is – Rebecca Brown, seat H25. Congratulations to Miss Brown. Announce yourself to one of the staff on duty with your ticket stub and proof of identity.'

Three jaws fell open and three pairs of eyes widened in shock.

"I think I'm going to faint," Rebecca announced. "Oh fuck, I've won, I've won. I can't believe it, I've won. We're going to meet him, we're actually going to meet him."

The three could hardly eat their takeaway due to their surprise and excitement at their coming meeting with their hero, which Rebecca had been told was scheduled to take place in six weeks. Those six weeks dragged by and all three went on crash diets and spent an inordinate amount of money on facials, fake tans and new clothes, much to the chagrin of their respective menfolk. When the day finally arrived, all three were packed and ready hours early. By the time the limo arrived, all three were more anxious and excited than they could remember being at any other time in their lives.

All Rebecca's neighbours were out to get a look as the three made their way to the waiting limo, dragging their suitcases behind them. Although only spending two nights away, each had packed enough for a week, after all, you need to be prepared for anything, right?

"Good evening ladies," the handsome blonde, blue eyed driver beamed as he opened the door for them. "Make yourselves comfortable. There's a bottle of champagne on ice inside, waiting for you. We'll be at your hotel in under two hours, then you'll check into your suite and have an hour to freshen up before I return to collect you for your dinner date with Mr Derran who is so excited to be sharing this weekend with you."

"Wow this is posh," Emma grinned as she settled back into the white leather upholstery.

"I'll have to get Rob to buy one of these," Beverlee laughed.

"Come on, get the champers out then," Rebecca winked.

"Need a bit of Dutch courage eh?" Emma teased.

They spent the journey discussing what Hank would be like in person as opposed to his movie persona and all agreed that he would most likely be cheeky, flirty and fun. Beverlee wondered if he would turn out to be a bit vain and Rebecca told her off for even thinking such a thing. One thing they were agreed on however, was that he was the best looking man they had ever set eyes on, so even if he turned out to have the IQ of a house brick, they would not care so long as they got a kiss and photo.

"What if he, y'know?" Beverlee asked.

"What?" Emma frowned.

"You know, what if he tries it on? Would you?"

"Hell yeah," Rebecca grinned, "wouldn't you?"

"Me first," Emma laughed.

"Hey, I won the competition so I get into his boxers."

"Share and share alike Hun," Beverlee responded. "You wouldn't have won if I hadn't got the tickets off Larry."

"That's true," Rebecca nodded, "but I get first go."

The conversation continued in a similar vein and by the time they arrived at their hotel, the driver was trying not to laugh. He had been secretly listening to his passengers' conversation on the intercom and had decided that it might be worth his while trying it on with them on the way home. They seemed like they would be keen enough, especially if he spun them a yarn about being Hank's personal driver and promised them tickets and more chances to meet him. He opened the door for them and gave them a wink as they stepped out of the limo and gazed up at the five star hotel in front of them. As the hotel doorman stepped forward to welcome them, he took a look at their legs and decided it would definitely be worth a shot on the way home.

"Welcome ladies," said the doorman as he stepped forward. "If you'd like to follow me, I'll get you checked in." He turned and waved to two young lads, who rushed forward for their suitcases.

The penthouse suite was the most sumptuous suite of rooms the three had ever seen and they spent a happy hour giggling as they unpacked and freshened up for their dinner date with the great Hank Derran. Right on cue, the receptionist called to inform them that their limo was waiting for them and would they please make their way to the lobby as soon as possible.

"Oh my god Beck," Emma screeched, "this is it. Dinner with Hank Derran."

"I'm sure I'll faint into the soup," Beverlee grinned.

"I'm too nervous to eat anything," Rebecca laughed.

They exited the lift and headed towards the lobby. As they rounded the corner, cameras flashed and everyone cheered. Rebecca almost jumped out of her skin and Emma put a hand to her chest in shock.

"Jeez, what's happening?" Beverlee hissed.

Before either of the others could reply, a tall man came towards them, arms open and expensive smile putting the camera flashes into the shade. All three girls stared into the face of Hank Derran, their jaws dropped and eyes wide. Emma put a hand to her mouth and almost burst into tears, Beverlee found to her horror that she was a little disappointed in the way he looked in the flesh as opposed to on screen and Rebecca almost passed out.

"Rebecca, my lovely," the smooth velvet voice crooned as the big arms enfolded her, crushing her into rock hard pectoral muscles. "How wonderful to meet you. Can I take you to dinner?" Rebecca could not speak, so she just nodded and Hank laughed at the cameras. Beverlee noticed how he was playing to the cameras and rolled her eyes discreetly. "Introduce me to your friends huh?" he grinned at Rebecca.

"This is Emma and this is Beverlee," she grinned, shy all of a sudden. Hank gave each one a hug for the cameras before encircling Rebecca's shoulder with one of his huge arms and slowly steering them towards a waiting group of TV reporters. Rebecca answered questions about how pleased she was to win the competition, how much she loved Hank's movies, and how excited they had all been for the past six weeks waiting for the big day.

"Tell me Rebecca," a thin man with a moustache asked. "When you entered the competition, what would you have given to ensure winning?"

Delectus Morbidium

"Anything," she grinned.

"Would you have sold your soul?" the man asked with a smile. Rebecca laughed and nodded.

"Yeah, absolutely."

The restaurant was obviously expensive but their table was discreetly placed so they could enjoy their meal without being unduly overlooked. The food was divine, the wine plentiful and the talk was all about Hank and his movies. Rebecca was hanging on his every word and he was taking full advantage. Emma, sat on Hank's other side, consoled herself with enjoying the way he continuously rubbed his knee against hers. Beverlee, who by this time had realised she didn't like him half as much in the flesh as she had in the movies, eyed up the guy sat at the table across the room whom she was sure she recognised from somewhere. Twice now he had looked over and smiled back at her and then a waiter had discreetly appeared with a small envelope and almost invisibly handed it to her. She opened it and found a phone number with a short message, – 'Hi Gorgeous, call me' and a smiley face. She was amazed and could not help but smile and look over at the guy, to find him gazing at her and smiling back. He mouthed "okay?" and nodded. She grinned and nodded back.

Four hours later the three were still giggling as they got ready for bed. Emma and Beverlee teased Rebecca mercilessly about how devoted she was to Hank and Emma shocked them all when she told them he had been rubbing his knee against hers throughout the meal and had twice put his hand on her thigh while no one was looking. Beverlee proudly showed them the note the cute guy from the table opposite had given her and all three agreed they had a good evening.

They had the whole of the next morning to themselves so they decided to go sightseeing and have some fun. After some shopping and a delicious lunch, they headed back to their hotel to wait for the limo to take them to the photo shoot. They arrived at the smart looking studio and were shown up to the fourth floor to meet with an unhealthily skinny and unnaturally blonde stylist for makeup and hair dressing. She

43

told them what would be happening during the shoot and encouraged them to relax and enjoy the whole thing. The three gulped in shock when they saw the fabulous range of clothes set aside for them. All the very best designers shared the rack and the stylist spent an hour discussing possible looks and helping them choose something that would bring out the best in them.

"We're all ready for you now ladies," a good looking young man with eyeliner and fake tan grinned. "If you'd all like to follow me."

Hank was there waiting for them, having brought along his own stylist, make up girl and hairdresser. Beverlee could not help but notice he looked older than in his movies; she saw definite lines at the corners of his eyes and a slight bagging of his upper eyelids. He looked tired, she thought.

"Rebecca my lovely," Hank crooned as he swept her into his arms. "The lady who would sell her soul to meet me, isn't she beautiful?" His 'people' as he introduced them all dutifully nodded and smiled and Beverlee groaned inwardly and tried not to grin as she caught Emma rolling her eyes at her. "Come on folks, I want my moment with Rebecca to be captured forever."

It was hard work trying to look relaxed and natural on camera and Emma found herself glad she had not obsessed about becoming a model when she was a teenager. Once the shots were taken, the photographer showed them to the girls on a computer so they could choose which ones they each wanted to take home. While they waited for their photos to be printed and framed, Hank took them down to the basement for coffee and a last chat before their time was over. He told them how much he had enjoyed meeting them and thanked them for being such devoted fans.

"And thank you for your soul Rebecca," he smiled as she giggled. "I'll take great care of it, I promise." He gave them each a signed photo and allowed them to take photos of him with them on their camera phones. The girls thanked him for giving his time to them and told him how much they had enjoyed meeting him. He gave them each a long, lingering kiss and hug before, framed photos in hand, they got up and headed out to the waiting limo for the trip back to the hotel to check out and the two hour drive home.

They decided to make use of the complimentary bottle of wine they found in their suite when they returned to pack and by the time they checked out and got into the limo, where they found another bottle of champagne like the one they enjoyed on the way up two days ago, they were laughing. Dusk was drawing in as the big limo headed south away from the city, but the intensifying fog didn't bother the girls; they were too busy giggling about Hank and his fake smile and wandering hands and Beverlee commented on his wrinkles.

"You don't see them in his movies," she announced.

"They're laughter lines," Rebecca retorted. "He smiles a lot."

"Rubbish," Emma laughed. "He's getting old, like all of us. The magic of digital manipulation is what we gawp at on screen."

Before anyone could reply, Rebecca was aware of a moment of painful noise that made no sense and seemed to come from everywhere at once. Then all was still and silent and she found herself standing at the side of the road in the fog. She could not remember how she got there; the last thing she could remember was laughing with Emma and Beverlee about Hank's wrinkles. What the fuck was going on?

"Rebecca?" The voice made her jump and she turned to find a mysterious man towering over her. He was handsome in a distinguished sort of way and he had an air of authority about him that she knew she must not ignore.

"Yes?" she answered with a frown. "What's happened and where are my friends? How did I get here? Where is the Limo?"

"It's time to go now Rebecca. Come with me."

"Go where?"

"Your friends survived the crash, they are okay. They'll say it was the fog, don't worry. We have to go now. You can't back out now, the deal has been done. This way." He gestured to his right and Rebecca looked. Out of the fog, she saw a glowing orange circle begin to appear and as she looked at it, it grew. Soon she realised it was not just an orange circle, it was a circle of fire. Raging flames leapt towards her and she flinched from them in terror.

"What's going on? What is this?" she begged the man but he remained impassive, still pointing towards the raging inferno in front of them.

"My client wanted a favour and I offered him a solution. You offered to pay and I accepted. My client has his wish and now it's time for us to go."

"What?" she yelled and tried to back away but found to her horror that she could not move. "Look I don't know what's going on but I have to get home now. I didn't make any deal nor did I offer to pay for anyone else's. Now where are my friends and who the fuck are you anyway?"

"My name is Lucifer. I am what you might call, the guy who can get what you want. Like any other business man, I don't work for nothing. My time is expensive but my service and my word is absolutely faultless. Mr Derran wanted a few more years of success before the ageing process slims down his career prospects and as you so kindly offered to pay the price of this deal, I am here to collect."

Rebecca frowned. "Hank? He wanted what? And what makes you think I offered to pay anything for him. I just don't get this. Is this some kind of sick joke by the magazine cos if it is, I'm getting really pissed off? I want my friends and I want to go home to my nice warm flat and boring job."

Lucifer sighed and shook his head as he gazed at Rebecca sadly. "Rebecca. Hank's not getting any younger and in the movie business, when you lose your looks, you're unemployable. He asked me to hold back the obvious ravages of time from his beautiful but enigmatic face for a few more years and I said yes. As I said before, I don't work for free and as you clearly stated to the national media, which I can replay for you if you've forgotten, you said you'd sell your soul for Hank. So, your limo unfortunately crashed in the fog, Hank is still handsome and you're coming with me." He took hold of her arm and squeezed.

Rebecca began to understand and Lucifer smiled as he read her thoughts.

"Yes my dear that is who I am." He laughed and as he did so, he dragged her screaming towards the entrance to hell.

THE END

FREESIAS FOR MANDY
starring Mandy Ward

Jerry bolted down the last of his sandwich. He was in a hurry tonight and nothing was going to delay him. He headed to his bathroom and switched the shower to medium warm, then strolled through to the bedroom to remove his clothes while the water heated. He hung his suit carefully in the closet to prevent it creasing, and so it would be ready to wear in the morning for his meeting with the board of Directors. He looked out his favourite jeans and Lacoste polo shirt in teal green and smiled; these would do perfectly for his date tonight. Not too formal yet not so casual as to appear slobbish. He was pleased with his choice and returned to his bathroom, whistling as he showered himself with the new exotic body wash he had treated himself to. The scent of Amber and Night Lily assailed his nostrils and he breathed deeply as he thought of the evening to come and his date with Mandy.

He met her at the office summer barbecue and they had clicked right away. He found her easy to talk to and uncomplicated, not like most of the other women he worked with who tended to be ruthlessly feminist and seemed to enjoy being as rude and obnoxious to men as they could. Not that he liked his women dumb, but he was not attracted to power hungry modern women like so many men of his age seemed to be. Mandy smiled a lot and always seemed grateful when anyone was friendly to her, and he never found her to be a threat to his masculinity. She liked reading and told him she wanted to write a book one day and he loved to hear her tell him stories she had made up. She liked Mexican food, collecting penguins and listening to Chopin. Jerry was hopelessly in love with her.

He stepped out of the shower, dried himself and took a long look at himself in the mirror. He ran a couple of blobs of styling gel through his hair before giving it a quick go over with the drier set on cold.

Moisturiser, a quick squirt of Amber and Night Lily body spray, a tidy up of the eyebrows and he smiled at his reflection.

"You look good buddy," he said and winked.

Jerry dressed quickly and decided on the dark tan boots in preference to the black. A leather jacket of the same dark tan hue, a cashmere scarf and he was ready. With a last look in the mirror, he locked his apartment door behind him and almost skipped downstairs to the parking garage where his Porsche sat gleaming in the strip lights. The sight of this car always made Jerry smile with satisfaction. He was not one for ostentatious shows of wealth; he preferred subdued elegance over flash and bling but this car was his one indulgence. Jet black and so shiny it always looked wet, Jerry loved the way this car made him feel as he cruised along. He kept his speed down, preferring to make sure everyone had time to see the car, and more importantly, him driving the car, rather than race around at top speed like a snotty nosed kid and annoy everyone. The admiration this car brought him pleased him, the understated way it showed his success without him having to be outwardly boastful.

The red light shined at the intersection and Jerry checked his Rolex; plenty of time yet, no need to hurry. A roar from his left caught his attention and he glanced across to see a bright red Ferrari occupied by three teenage boys who did not look old enough to be out this late, let alone drive such a car as that. They leered at him, laughed between themselves and the driver jazzed the gas pedal continuously, obviously offering him a race. He laughed to himself and thought back to when he was that age and already working his way up through the ranks of the family business. The light turned green and he ignored them as the kid pressed his sneaker to the floor and stalled the Ferrari. Jerry laughed loudly as he cruised away and headed for the freeway out of the city.

Once out of the city, Jerry relaxed and switched on the cd player. Bruce Springsteen yelled at the top of his voice and he could not help but join in. Together, the two of them brought the thousands of screaming fans to hysteria at Madison Square Garden. Mandy was not

Delectus Morbidium

that keen on Bruce Springsteen but Jerry did not mind. He could not make head nor tail of Chopin so he reckoned that made them even, and he believed it gave them something to talk about. One thing they did have in common was an expensive taste in coffee, and he loved to scour the internet looking for strange and obscure sources of unknown blends for them to try and critique, and they had both become quite educated in the whole subject of coffee. From the ideal environmental conditions for the growing plants, to the optimum harvest time of the beans and the best blend and roast, they debated and tried them all.

The freeway exit loomed and Jerry headed into the countryside. As he drove the deserted lanes, Bruce began a love song and Jerry's thoughts turned to the wonderful moment when he had first made love to Mandy. He enjoyed wooing a woman before going to bed with her and for him it was all part of foreplay. Great pleasure could be enjoyed in the accidental brushing of his hand on her arm and the close, but not too close, embrace he gave her when they danced. One of the most important habits he believed in, was to make sure he took her flowers; nothing showy or gauche but always sweet smelling. Violets, sweet peas or freesia were his favourites, never roses or, heaven forbid, orchids. Those were for gropers, fumblers and unsophisticated louts with beer on their breath and cheap condoms in their pockets; bought in value packs in the late night drugstore.

That first night, he took her to the very spot they were meeting tonight and lay on the autumn leaves gazing up at the heavens. It was obvious to Jerry that this was the moment; that she was happy and compliant was obvious, and he savoured every moment as he slowly undressed her and saw how her skin seemed to glow in the moonlight. He felt a tingle in his crotch as he remembered the shuddering climax she afforded him that night and was hopeful of another tonight. As he turned off the empty road into the National Park parking lot, he was so hard that it was painful and he had to restrain himself from masturbating.

Locking the Porsche, he headed down the path, the small posy of freesias smelling sweetly in the still night air. Entering the cover of the trees, he took a moment to allow his eyes to adjust to the gloom before heading on down the steep incline and hopping over the small stream that ran along the bottom. Halfway up the other side, the almost invisible trail led off to his right and he held the freesias to his nose as he made his way along and allowed their scent to remind him of her. Five hundred yards in, he bent under the fallen tree and carefully picked his way through the thicket behind and there she was, waiting for him.

"Hello beautiful," he smiled as he gazed down at her. "I've brought you freesias tonight, I hope you like them." He knelt down beside her and gazed into her eyes. His eyes brimmed with tears as he allowed his overwhelmimg love for her to overtake him, and as he allowed his hand to trace its way up her thigh to her crotch, he felt his own body responding.

"Oh baby I love you so much," he gasped as he teased his fingers between her panties and her thigh and felt the softness within. "I want you Mandy, I want you baby." His voice was just a whisper as he pulled down her panties and unzipped himself. With a sigh of desire, he kissed her deeply as he entered her and began to thrust. He knew he would not last long tonight; he was so overwhelmed with desire for her that their first coupling of the night was always a quick and urgent affair. Their later, subsequent lovemaking sessions would be slow and sensual and it really turned him on to climax with her as the sun broke over the distant horizon after a whole night out here under the stars.

Jerry felt his climax approaching and began to grunt as he thrusted hard. With one last thrust he exploded inside her and then felt something give way underneath him. When his passion was spent, he looked down and sighed with disappointment.

"Oh no baby, not already," he said with tears in his eyes. He climbed off, dressed himself and went to retrieve her panties. He managed to get them to the top of her thighs before the right hip bone came away with a sickening squish and sent the whole right leg canting away at an unnatural angle. The night birds screeched overhead as he looked down at her once delicate pubic mound and smiled sadly. That sweet mound that had given him such pleasure now wriggled and writhed as the maggots fed. He bent and kissed her mouth, letting his tongue dance over hers for one last time and as her lower jawbone fell away, he stood and turned to go.

"I'm sorry Mandy, but it's not working between us. It's over baby," he said quietly as he picked his way through the thicket and stooped under the fallen tree.

THE END

LOVE ETERNAL
starring Rob Clague & David John McVie

Rob cleared his throat and sighed, readying his best telephone voice before lifting the receiver, silencing the annoying trill. Once again, he mentally promised to set the phone to a new, and hopefully less annoying, ring tone.

"Good morning, RB Clague Funeral Home. How can we be of service?"

He listened, jotting down notes where necessary and being sympathetic as she sobbed her way through the conversation. Once he talked her into coming in at three to discuss the details, he gave her his condolences and rang off. Walking through to the back, he called to his assistant.

"Dave? Hey Dave, where are you?"

"Over here Boss," a voice called from the corner.

Rob watched as Dave McVie stood, his face streaked with dirt and the remains of a cobweb dangling from one ear.

"Just tidying up a bit," he grinned. "What's the problem?"

"I have a client coming in this afternoon at three, so have a few different caskets on display will ya?"

"Sure."

"Oh, and clean yourself up a bit too," Rob said as he turned to go. "She's just lost her daughter so we have to be extra sensitive with this one."

"No problem at all," Dave grinned.

Rob expertly steered a distraught Mrs Parker through all the details necessary to ensure her daughter's funeral would be a fitting tribute to a much loved young woman. He continuously assured her that he and his company would take care of everything so she would have no need to worry and was delighted to be able to help her choose one of the more expensive caskets they had to offer. After recommending Cynthia's Floral Tributes in the unit three doors down, he shook hands with her and showed her out.

Jenny Parker, or at least her bodily remains, arrived at RB Clague Funeral Home late that afternoon, Rob and Dave having picked her up from the morgue in their large black van.

"This is gonna be a closed casket Dave," Rob said. "Damn shame too, such a pretty gal."

"I guess she was before that truck rearranged everything," Dave snickered and Rob scowled.

"Shut the fuck up you asshole."

"Sorry Boss, just a little workplace humour."

"The funeral is next Tuesday morning at ten, in Rose Garden Cemetary."

"Rose Garden?" Dave said. "That's a little out of the way isn't it? Why there?"

"It's near where the family lived when Jenny was a kid and her mother says she loved to go in there and look at the angel statues. Apparently she once said she would like to be there when she died, so her mother wants her planted there. We'll have to leave a good hour for the trip, so we have to leave the shop no later than nine okay? You'll have her ready in time?"

"Have I ever let you down Boss?" Dave asked. He enjoyed his work and often worked late into the night, long after his boss, Rob, had gone home to his wife and kids.

After getting her washed down and prepared for embalming, Dave realised that apart from a broken neck and smashed face, a few broken ribs, one of which had sliced her heart in two, the rest of her was in good shape. It had been several months since he had a beautiful young girl to work with and he let his hand take hold of her breast. They were full, the nipples dark and as he flicked his tongue over them, his hand found the auburn fluff of pubic hair and the cold inviting darkness between her legs.

Delectus Morbidium

She was tight around him as he thrust into her and despite the coldness of her body, he knew he wouldn't be able to contain himself for long. This was the most pleasure he had been able to enjoy in months; the obese middle aged housewives and elderly widows who usually passed through the workshop, not gripping half as tightly around his penis as Jenny was now doing. The last one had been seventy three when she turned up in the workshop after a stroke took her from her equally elderly husband. Her breasts had been flat as pancakes and it had taken him nearly ten minutes of pumping her flabby insides in order for him to come. He christened her Sally Slack after that and had almost said the name aloud to Rob when they were getting her into the hearse for the ride to the graveyard.

Dave finally dragged himself home at three in the morning, after enjoying Jenny's body in every conceivable way and in every possible position he could think of. He grinned as he looked at the photographs he'd taken of Jenny and himself, before taking a quick shower and going to bed. Next morning he was up bright and early and despite the lack of sleep, he was at work early and took the risk of enjoying Jenny's delights one more time before Rob turned up to open the shop. By the time Rob unlocked and made the coffee, Jenny's embalming was well under way.

Once the embalming was completed, her body was stored in the refrigerator to await her funeral. Even though hers was to be a closed casket, the family still visited daily and spent over an hour sitting beside the shiny pink casket, talking of her childhood and looking at all the family photographs taken of her since the day she was born. Every night, Dave would sneak back to the workshop and spend hours with her body. One night he fell asleep on top of her as she lay in her coffin, his penis still buried inside her cold body. He awoke at three thirty five and thought it was the horniest thing he had ever experienced and continued having sex with her until five. The fat old bags that usually passed through the funeral home normally got Dave's attention no more than once or twice but he could not get enough of young Jenny and more than once, he thought of stealing her body and keeping her at his home.

The day of the funeral arrived and Dave was at work well before anyone else. He wanted one last liaison with his new love and he enjoyed every second of it. He stripped off and climbed into the casket, lifted her legs and let them dangle over the sides and fell on her, the desire coursing through his body. His tongue found her cold nipples as he began to thrust and he was so driven by his fast approaching orgasm, that he did not notice the door open and a figure enter. Dave groaned as he banged his hips into hers and felt his balls begin to squeeze. His groans of pleasure more than adequately covered the sounds of the soft footsteps that padded towards the coffin and his last thought as his penis exploded inside Jenny's dead body, was to wonder what that sudden pain in his head was.

Rob dropped the sledge hammer to the floor and quickly set about locking down the lid of the casket. A couple of phone calls later, his brothers and two cousins arrived to help with the funeral.

"Damn nuisance Dave just leaving like this, and on the day of a funeral too," he said to his brother Adam.

"Well if you need another assistant, I might be able to help you out. I'm between jobs right now and I know what to do."

"You haven't forgotten what Dad taught us, after seven years in an office?" Rob joked.

"Hell no," Adam grinned. "After growing up in the funeral business, you never forget. I was helping Dad embalm when I was ten years old and did one on my own at thirteen."

"I was fourteen and a half," Rob replied. "If you want it, the job is yours. You gotta respect the dead though, no funny stuff with the pretty young girls that come in. And some of them are pretty. Some are gorgeous and sexy women."

"Hey, what do you take me for?" Adam said and they both laughed.

Delectus Morbidium

Six hours later, Dave awoke with a searing pain in his head and realised that not only was it pitch black, but that he couldn't breathe very well. He felt the body beneath him and realised he was still buried up to his balls inside Jenny Parker. It took a few seconds for all the threads to come together into one recognisable whole, and when it did, Dave screamed. It took him two days to die of suffocation and in that time, he had sex with Jenny another five times.

Rob cleared his desk and went to lock up the shop. He strolled back to his office and flicked on his computer. A few taps and a password brought up the closed circuit television cameras he had secretly installed four months ago. He went first to the file dated twelve weeks ago and sat back and watched his ex-assistant Dave have sex with the dead body of a girl of twelve. He then flipped forward three weeks and watched him with Milly Robinson, the thirty two year old bus driver. Finally he flipped forward and watched him with Jenny Parker and as he saw him taking her body from behind, her head and shoulders propped up on some boxes of embalming chemicals, Rob's own body shuddered as he felt the slick wet in his hand.

THE END

59

JOURNEY
starring Theresa O'Neill and Mark Lewis

Theresa tried to move into a more comfortable position. It was difficult as things were getting tight in there now. She knew she had put on weight and would probably continue to do so. She groaned as she realised she was beginning to regret going along with the advice from her mentor. She did what she did so often now, and thought back to when her life was carefree and filled with wonder. She was so happy back then and it seemed that there was nothing in existence that could wipe the smile from her face, nor the joy from her heart. That was before, of course. Before, this.

She would never forget that day she got the first inkling that things were going to change for her, and change for the worse. She had a job she enjoyed, looking after the sick, and she was good at it. A natural healer her mentor had so often said and Theresa knew it was true. She loved seeing people get better and get back to full energy again. It made her feel useful, needed, and it gave her existence a worthy purpose.

She remembered the young man who had been in a motorcycle crash. He was so traumatised, it took months to rehabilitate him but as always, Theresa was patient and encouraging and her heart was overflowing with joy when she watched him leave with a smile on his face. Mark, that was his name, Mark Lewis. Then there was Alexa, the woman who had come in after a routine operation. She had been difficult at times, Theresa remembered, but the woman had a fighting spirit and she admired that in people. She hadn't enjoyed being there and had been quite sharp with Theresa on a number of occasions but as always, her love and encouragement soon worked miracles.

Her mentor had called her aside one day and Theresa knew from the look in her eyes that she wasn't going to like what she had to say.

"I'm sorry Theresa but you have to leave us soon."

"Leave, but why?" Theresa wailed, her mouth agape.

"You can't stay here forever, we told you that when you first started here. It wasn't ever going to be a permanent arrangement."

"But," Theresa began.

"But nothing Theresa. Come on now, you knew this day would come and you said you understood and were happy with it. You can't back out now anyway, the arrangements for your replacement have already been made."

"How long have I got till I have to go?" Theresa asked sadly.

"A week or so. Your counsellor will help you make the necessary arrangements. He will contact you within a day or so."

Theresa's heart ached with sadness at the knowledge that she would have to leave soon. It was true, she had known all along that this wasn't going to be a permanent arrangement here. This day had always seemed so far away in the future though and she hadn't thought about it. She had allowed herself to think it would never happen but now it had and it was a shock. She went back to her work but struggled to find her smile and several of her patients picked up on her sadness and asked her if she was all right. She managed to lie to them pretty convincingly though and hoped her sadness wouldn't put their own recovery back.

She hauled her leg from under her, desperate to find a comfortable position and tried not to think about how she was to get out of here. She looked up and saw the tiny entrance hole and gulped. She looked away, not wanting to think about the pain involved in trying to get her body through that small gap. Why the hell did she allow herself to get stuck in here for so long? What was she thinking when she agreed to this? She forced her mind away and thought back to the conversation she had with her counsellor. She had found him to be pleasant and helpful and didn't hesitate to trust him. How she wished she had followed her own mind and not let him persuade her to get into this predicament. If she ever saw him again, he was going to pay, and pay dearly.

Delectus Morbidium

"Now Theresa," he said with that soft voice she trusted. "Your time of leaving us is drawing near and we must prepare for your journey."

"Where will I be going?" she asked.

"You will be going to live with a couple named O'Neill. They are very nice and will look after you so don't worry."

"Okay," she nodded.

Over the days leading up to her time of departure, she had asked him all sorts of questions and he had patiently answered them all and led her to believe that she was to have a wonderful time. It was a new start, he said. A time of celebration he said. They will be so pleased to see you, he said. Like an idiot, she hadn't suspected a thing until the time came for her to actually begin her journey and she saw how she was to travel.

"You mean I have to be locked inside that tiny space?" she exclaimed in horror.

"Now now Theresa stop panicking. It's warm and comfortable and has everything you need for your journey. You can lie back and relax and not worry about a thing."

"But you know I get claustraphobic," she wailed.

"That will soon pass once you relax into it," he assured her. "Now come on, there's a good girl, hop in."

So she took a deep breath and stepped inside. At first she panicked but soon she became used to it and it didn't seem so bad as she had first thought. That was before she put on so much weight though and now it was just plain uncomfortable and she wanted out. The trouble was, she was now far too big for that small entrance hole and she feared she was to be a prisoner here forever. Maybe she could force her way out some other way, she thought and began to kick and punch all around her. Maybe there is a weak spot somewhere and with a concerted effort, she might be able to break out and run away.

At times she thought she heard voices, muffled and far away but she couldn't make out the words. There was one woman she heard more than any other voice and a man too who was nearby quite often.

63

She screamed at them to let her out but they obviously couldn't hear her, or were just ignoring her. Probably the latter, she thought miserably. She spent long hours alternately feeling unhappy and trying to bash her way out. Neither did any good and just made her tired so when she wasn't feeling sad or trying to fight her way out of her prison, she slept very uncomfortably.

One day, she was awoken by an agonising pain. It felt as if her whole body were being crushed. She tried to cry out in pain but no sound came. She felt her bones bending with each rhythmic crush and felt sure she was going to die in horrible agony. This went on for hours and she wailed in agony and begged to be set free. She yelled her apologies for whatever it was she had done to deserve such punishment and she promised never to do it again if they just let her out. No one heard, or no one cared and the painful crushing continued unabated. Suddenly she felt something on the top of her head. A coldness that she hadn't felt before gripped her and she instinctively tried to withdraw from it but the incessant crushing prevented any escape. Without warning she felt her whole body rush from her prison into glorious freedom. She screamed out her anguish at her long imprisonment and listened as a new voice, loud and clear this time, boomed from above.

"Congratulations Mrs O'Neill, it's a little girl."

Theresa felt warm hands caress her, soothing words reached her ears and wonderful, all consuming love surrounded her. She sucked greedily and let the memories of all those brave souls whom she had nursed back to spiritual health after the death of their physical bodies, withdraw into the mist.

THE END

MEET THE PARENTS
starring Brandy Edwards

Oh I'm so tired, I can hardly keep my eyes open. I feel I need to close them, to allow my mind to drift off, somewhere. Where? I don't care, anywhere but here. Hey there little fella, where did you come from? It's so nice to have company at last. What's your name buddy? I'm Brandy, pleased to meet ya. How long have you been sitting there? I didn't notice you when I arrived but then I was so happy that I didn't notice a lot of things I should've noticed. Hey you know what? It's my eighteenth birthday today. My boyfriend Dexter said he was going to throw me a party at his grandparent's house to celebrate my special day and to introduce me to his folks at last. I was so excited and felt really grown up to be finally getting to meet Dexter's folks.

Dexter's family keep themselves to themselves. They're very private y'know? I met him while I was walking my dog Eddy through the woods six months ago and he was walking his own dog. First time I saw him I thought, wow this guy is gorgeous and when his dog came running over to meet Eddy I was so blown away by him that I got all tongue tied and blushed like a silly kid. He was nice though and pretty soon we were chatting like old friends and he asked if I'd mind if he joined Eddy and me on our walk. Would I mind? Are you crazy?

After that I used to walk Eddy in the woods every day and it became a habit for Dexter to meet us there and walk with us. I looked forward to those walks and pretty soon I was beginning to wonder if anything would happen between us. The boys at school are nice enough but not a patch on Dexter and I used to daydream about seeing all my girlfriends' faces when they met him for the first time. You know it took him a whole month before he tried to kiss me? How cute is that? After that he would hold my hand while we walked and I felt like his real girlfriend, it was awesome.

Three months after our first meeting, he asked me if I would be his girlfriend and I said yes. He kissed me with his tongue for the first time and my insides did a flip flop. Man I was so happy that day. Have you had something like that happen buddy? No? That's a shame, that's a real shame. I asked him to come to the diner with me one weekend and meet some of my friends but he said no. He must've seen I was upset as he held me in his arms and told me he loved me for the first time and said he didn't want to share me with anyone just yet, that he wanted me all to himself for just a little longer and that he'd like me to meet his folks. I was okay with that because Sandy told me that if a boy takes you to meet his folks, then it's a serious relationship.

He knew my eighteenth birthday was just a month away so he said him and his folks were arranging a party for me, so they could all meet me and we could celebrate my birthday together and be like a family. I was so nervous this afternoon when I was getting ready. I'd never been taken to meet a boyfriend's parents before and I wasn't sure what I should wear. Normally I'd wear something real, y'know revealing, but I reckoned that if his folks were anything like mine, then they probably wouldn't approve of me having too much bare flesh on show. Parents can be such old farts can't they? Are yours like that?

I finally settled on a bright red dress with a sweetheart neckline and tight skirt that came down to just above the knees. I'd seen a movie where the heroine wore an identical dress and then a week later I saw this in the boutique on main street so I bought it. Mom took the hem up for me and Cassie from next door did my make up. Her older sister is at beauty college so she gets to use all the top brands of cosmetics and Cassie always looks a million dollars as her sister taught her how to do her own face properly. I wore my sneakers and carried my red heels, as I was going through the woods to meet Dexter and didn't want to get them all muddy and Mom said that kind of shoe is made for posing, not walking. My dad bought me a second hand car and I was totally blown away by it and Mom said she'd pay for me to have lessons and get my driver's license. I was so happy when I left the house this afternoon and set off through the woods and when I saw Dexter waiting for me in his dark suit and bow tie I was like, wow.

He told me I looked beautiful and kissed me and I thought this was the happiest day of my life. Then he handed me a small box and said happy birthday baby. It was a solid gold necklace with a big heart shaped red stone that he said was some kind of ancient crystal that had magical properties in the country his grandparents came from. We walked holding hands and every so often he'd stop and pull me close and kiss me and say thank you for giving yourself to me and making me so happy. I was hoping that tonight was gonna be the night when he'd finally, y'know, do it.

It must've taken nearly an hour of walking before Dexter pulled me off the path along an almost invisible track and then there it was. The house wasn't quite what I'd expected his folks to live in. It was old and looked like it needed a paint job and a few repairs here and there but the lights shone in the downstairs windows and he led me up to the front door where a huge banner hung outside. I couldn't read what it said but my name Brandy was in the middle so I guessed it was some kind of happy birthday greeting. Dexter said it was the language his grandparents used before they came to this country and he said it was a greeting to me.

"Brandy?" he smiled at me. "It's traditional in my grandparent's culture for the girl to knock on the door and ask to come in."

"Really?" I blushed and he nodded.

"Yeah. It's okay baby don't be shy. Just knock and when they answer the door, say I'm Brandy and I want to come in and give myself to Dexter. It's just an old fashioned thing that brings luck on a relationship and it would make them so happy. They're a little shy since they're foreigners here and they'd love it if you showed them you don't think they're traditions are weird or anything. Please baby, for me huh?" He kissed me and I couldn't refuse him, even though it seemed mighty weird to me so I knocked and waited. The door was opened by a little wrinkled old lady with the strangest glow in her eyes I'd ever seen. She said something in a language I didn't understand so I smiled and held tight to Dexter's hand.

"Hello, I'm Brandy and I want to come in and give myself to Dexter," I blushed and looked at him. He winked at me and the old lady smiled and opened the door and waved us in. The inside of the house was warm and smelled of spices and I could hear a fire crackling somewhere. A man appeared and came up to me with a smile as he introduced himself as Dexter's grandfather. He thanked me for accepting their traditions and asked me if I was happy to be Dexter's chosen girl. I smiled and nodded and he offered me a drink which tasted funny but I didn't want to be rude and say I didn't like it so I just drank it down.

That's where it all begins to get a bit hazy for me. I must've fallen asleep or something because I remember a really vivid dream of being chained to a table. I was naked and had symbols painted on my skin and I could hear voices chanting and singing all around me. Then Dexter appeared in the dream and he was naked too and he climbed on top of me and started to make love to me. I was just beginning to enjoy it when he started talking in my ear as we were, y'know, doing it. I couldn't understand what he was saying but his voice became different somehow, scary. I looked at him and this is where the dream gets seriously crazy. His eyes weren't like they normally are. They were bright orange and as I looked at him, he changed from the gorgeous brown eyed young man I knew, into this orange eyed, hairy creature with huge fangs and as his body started jerking, he bit down into my neck. It hurt so much and I screamed and then the dream must've gone because I don't remember any more until I woke up here chained to this bed and saw you here. I'm so tired, I think I'll just sleep awhile. You will be here when I wake up won't you? It's so nice having you to talk to.

The door opened and the old lady entered, followed by the elderly man. She looked at the imp guarding the chosen one and raised her eyebrows questioningly. The imp bowed his head to the old woman.

"Her time is near, Mistress. I can feel the dark lord's successor preparing to make his entrance into this human world at last."

"Good," the old woman nodded. "It has been too much trouble keeping her alive this past year. When will he be with us?"

"Before the sun rises Mistress, the dark lord will have his successor at last." The imp bowed again as the old woman smiled and left the room to make preparations.

Throughout the long hours of the night the body of the earth female lay writhing in its agonies as the dark lord's successor fought its way out. The old woman and old man stood impassively watching, unmoved as her screams split the night air. Just before the sun rose over the distant horizon, the dark lord appeared and waited for his newborn son to arrive. The old man and woman bowed reverently to him and stepped aside, allowing him to come forward and wait to receive the child into his own hands. The body of the female began to writhe and scream afresh as the belly began to tear open. Blood gushed onto the bed as a tiny clawed hand appeared from within the gash.

"Welcome my son," the dark lord cried. "Welcome into this world where you will have dominion over all." He leaned forward and reached out his hands as the tiny claw ripped the belly of its host open. The head appeared from within the bloody rent, its tiny horn buds glistening with blood and let out a loud wailing cry. The dark lord smiled as he took his newborn son into his arms and looked down at him. His tears fell upon the newborn's face as his old heart swelled with love.

THE END

Merita King

OUT OF CHARACTER

starring Mike Wall, Jeany Williamson & Linda Sloan Whitten

The clock struck six pm and Mike put down his beer. His eyes widened a little before rolling back into his head as the now familiar buzzing began, right in the centre of his brain. He'd learned some time ago that it was useless trying to fight it and that the information would come through much more clearly defined if he relaxed and just let it flow. As the buzzing reached its most painful frequency, the images began and he absorbed them all in as much detail as he was able. This time it was a woman, alone in what looked like a parking lot at night and fumbling in the dark for her car keys. He noticed buildings nearby but couldn't make out what they were but that didn't matter, he could fill in those less important details himself. The woman was named Linda and Mike thought she was pretty, so pretty in fact that if he met her in real life, he'd have little hesitation in asking her out. Then he heard a voice he recognised and he smiled. There was only one man who had that voice, Roy Gilquist, Mike's fictional serial killer.

"Excuse me ma'am." Mike watched as the image of the woman Linda jumped in surprise and turned around, a hand going instinctively to her breast as she registered the man twenty yards away and coming towards her.

"Are you Linda Whitten?" the voice of Roy asked the frightened woman, who nodded. "You dropped your driver's licence in the store. Here." Mike felt rather than saw, Roy smiling as he continued approaching Linda, his hand outstretched, something clearly held between his slim fingers.

"Oh," Linda sighed with relief. "Thank you so much," she replied as she voluntarily closed the gap between them and reached out to take the blank piece of paper that masqueraded as her driver's licence.

Mike grinned as he felt the excitement flood through Roy's body and settle into his groin in the familiar first flush of sexual arousal, the beginning of an erection as her hand touched his fingers, the aching hardness as his hands gripped her throat and the warmth of release as the life left her frightened eyes. He watched from inside his mind as Roy gently laid her down in the far corner of the parking lot, away from the lights and the threat of passer's by and began to cut and slice. The taste of warm blood filled Mike's mouth as Roy chewed and swallowed, the flesh as solid and real to him as any he might find in his own refrigerator. As Roy's feast ended, the darkness descended into Mike's mind and he slept. Twenty minutes later he awoke and as always, headed straight to his den to write down the story.

Mike had been half-heartedly writing horror stories for a while but it wasn't until he started chronicling the misadventures of Roy Gilquist, the half man half demon serial killer that he got a real passion for writing. It was also Roy's appearance that had signalled the start of what Mike called 'the buzz,' which was how he described the way the stories came to him. The pain in his temple, the buzzing noise and then the images which at first had sickened him and as always, the sleep for twenty minutes, after which he would have to immediately write down what he'd seen or the same images would return that same night in his dreams, only this time more painful than he found bearable. It seemed the more he tried to fight it, the worse it got and the only way to get through was to give in and write it.

One hundred and forty two miles away, Police Officer Jeany Williamson put a hand over her mouth and groaned at the sight. The handsome forensic guy Doug smiled at her apologetically and stood.

"Okay Doug, what do we have?"

"Linda Sloane Whitten, fifty two years old. Office worker for a firm of architects. That's her car behind you by the way. My professional opinion is death by strangulation. The cutting of the body was done post mortem. I'd say she's been dead no longer than five or six hours."

Delectus Morbidium

"Is it the same as the others?"

"I'd say so yeah."

"Anything missing this time?"

"Yep, part of the liver and the left eyeball."

"So I can presume it's the same guy?"

"You can indeed. I've finished with her for now. She's all yours. You'll have the autopsy report within twenty four hours."

"Thanks Doug."

"No problem. Still on for dinner on Friday?"

"Sure thing. Want me to bring dessert?"

"Delightful, but not chocolate okay? You know how it affects me."

Back in his own quiet backwater town, Mike typed furiously into the small hours documenting every last detail of Roy Gilquist's latest adventure into the disgustingly macabre. Stretching his aching back, he got up and wandered through to his kitchen to get himself another beer and enjoy a cigarette on the porch before hitting the sack. Having lost his job six months ago he had plenty of time on his hands to indulge his new passion for horror writing. As the night birds called overhead, his thoughts turned to finance and the ever present worry about how he was to survive without a job. This town offered zero possibilities for employment for guys of his age. His prospects were grim and with his savings dwindling fast he knew he had to find an income from somewhere soon or he'd be a street bum before next Christmas. When he wasn't writing, Mike went for long drives in his battered pickup truck and knew the area for three hundred miles around like the back of his hand. He'd park up somewhere and go for a walk with his battered camera and twice had photographs bought by magazines. There was a time when he'd thought perhaps his financial problems could be solved by his love of photography but he'd quickly realised that was not to be. Without better equipment or the money to buy it, he didn't stand a chance in today's market.

It was as he flipped his cigarette butt into the dirt that the thought occurred to him that he might be able to make money out of writing horror books. He knew that his Roy Gilquist stories were good, very good in fact and with his old but trusty laptop he could publish his own work and sell online. The old gal from the corner store sold a few books to the regular crop of tourists who passed through town and he knew of an old guy who published his own books on local history and legends. Maybe if he bought him a few beers next time he saw him, he might give him some tips on how to do it.

"If that old buzzard can do it, then it can't be beyond me," he said aloud. "Roy Gilquist, I'm gonna make you famous my friend, and get rich into the bargain. Win win for both of us huh?" he laughed out loud and raised his almost empty bottle in toast. "Here's to Hell's Justice, starring Roy Gilquist, half man half demon serial killer and written by soon to be rich and famous Mike Wall." Still laughing to himself, he left the now empty bottle on the porch and went in to bed. Halfway up the stairs a sound caught his attention and made him stop, his right leg in mid stride. It sounded like a creaking floorboard, almost as if someone were walking across one of the rooms above and hadn't quite managed to keep his footsteps quiet. He listened for a few seconds before shaking his head and yawning; he must be imagining things. He opened the bathroom, unzipping himself and took a pee, before turning to the basin to brush his teeth. The toothpaste was cold and he winced as his sensitive tooth complained.

As he bent to spit and rinse he saw the shadow fall across the tiled floor behind him, and his heart fluttered in his chest as fear coursed through his body. The realisation that someone was standing right behind him in his own bathroom made his head swim, and for several seconds he was too afraid to stand up and turn around. He didn't want to come face to face with an intruder in his own home when he had nothing to hand with which to defend himself, and wasn't even sure he'd have the presence of mind to use a weapon in a real situation anyway. He almost burst into tears and thought back to when he was a kid afraid of the dark and cried for his mother to come and hold him and keep him safe. He wished he were five years old again and could call out for Mom to come and make everything better.

Despite all these thoughts rushing through his mind within a few seconds, Mike stood and turned around, eyes wide with terror and faced the source of the shadow. His mouth fell open in shock as he saw the familiar rugged countenance and gazed into those cold grey eyes he'd come to know so well.

"Roy?" he hissed in disbelief. "It can't be. You're a figment of my imagination. I'm going mad, you're not real." He squeezed his eyes shut for a few seconds but when he opened them, the face that met his gaze now grinned mockingly.

"Oh but we are," the man in front of him replied, his voice mellow and slow. The kind of voice that would melt women's hearts. "At least half of us is."

"But," Mike began. "But how? Why? Half of you?"

"The human half, the Roy half. We've been looking for you for months," Roy Gilquist replied.

"You have, why?"

"You've been spying on us, haven't you Mike. We've felt you, rummaging around inside our mind and watching the show."

"But that's ridiculous," Mike exclaimed. "I'm a writer and you're just my imagination."

"We don't know how you do it but we can't have you shuffling around in here," Roy continued, tapping a slender finger to his temple. "Not in our line of work. And after trespassing inside our head and getting your private kicks out of us, you're going to repay us by shopping us and our work to the general public. That's not very nice. We like our privacy. It took me a long time to find a human host as compliant as Roy and I'm not ready to let him go just yet. Have you any idea how careful we have to be when melding with a human host? Have you?"

Mike shook his head. "No, sorry."

"The average human body could literally explode when a demon like myself enters them and tries to take control. We have to choose

75

carefully and take our time with the blending. And then you come along and try to fuck things up for us. That makes us very angry and now we have to teach you a lesson."

Mike was aware of heat as Roy's hands clasped him around the throat and began to squeeze. The heat grew in intensity until he felt he was literally on fire. He tried to scream in fright and pain but no sound would come, his throat too constricted by those strong hands. The smell of burning flesh came next and just before Mike passed out, he was vaguely aware of flames eating away at his face and neck.

The fire consumed everything within the small house, burning everything within to ash. All of Mike's carefully typed stories, the work of months in ashes ensuring Roy Gilquist and his demon passenger their privacy. Roy Gilquist smiled to himself as he watched the chaos ensue. Firemen ran around shouting but were unable to control the blaze, or save the life of the owner. All that remained of Mike was three of his teeth, which the local police used to identify him and the empty beer bottle that remained unharmed, a silent toast to evil still standing on what remained of the back porch.

Roy's excitement grew as the terrified woman registered what was about to happen to her, and it was as he watched the last dregs of her life force leave, that he felt the familiar stirrings inside the mind he shared with his host. Someone was watching, listening, sharing the experience.

THE END

SPOTLIGHTS AND SCREAMS

starring Santosh Kumar & Hannah Tate

He reached over and switched off the radio, frowning as the opening bars of the all too familiar song reached his ears.

"No thank you Miss Tate, not today. Not any day," he muttered as he dialled another station and smiled as the smooth piano melody filled his kitchen. "That's much better."

Taking a swig from his coffee mug, he grimaced. It was cold again and he mentally admonished himself for forgetting it. As it reheated in the microwave, he wandered over to the front door and picked up his newspaper. The weekly Hanson column made him laugh as usual; he had really come to admire Dick Hanson for his satire and his comical way of looking at the topical political issues of the day. A two page article on government spending cuts got no more than a passing glance and a groan of boredom, so he flipped the page and read all about an undercover operation by four reporters into mistreatment of elderly residents in nursing homes around the country. In the arts section, he read the reviews of the latest John Mack novel and decided to buy it when he was next in town. Then the music section caught his eye and he frowned again. She was coming to town.

"Well I won't be bothering to come and listen to your unearthly caterwauling," he said aloud. Up until six months ago he'd been a huge fan of Hannah Tate, the world famous jazzy ballad singer with the husky voice that reminded him just a little of Eartha Kitt. He'd travelled across the world to see her perform live and hadn't begrudged a penny of it; until she'd come to London that is. After the London gig he hated her and would never listen to her again. The rain had soaked right through his coat, shirt and vest and as he hopped from foot to foot to keep the blood flowing to his frozen toes, he felt his sodden socks squelch inside his shoes. That didn't bother him though and had there been a blizzard or a hurricane, he'd still have waited there with a smile on his face because she was coming out soon and he'd get to see her, maybe even get a hello and a photograph.

After three hours his patience had been rewarded as the rather unremarkable back door of the theatre opened and half a dozen burly minders emerged, flanking the vision of beauty and creative talent that he adored. Four huge black umbrellas held aloft by the minders kept her dry as they ushered her down the three steps and out to the limo that waited, its engine almost silent. The other fans surged forward, pushing and shoving each other as they called her name but Santosh was clever and held back. He waited near the limo and knew that once the throng had what they wanted, he'd have her attention as she got into her car.

A minder, easily seven feet tall and the same wide, shoved Santosh aside and yanked open the offside rear door of the black limo. Almost stumbling onto the soaked tarmac, Santosh managed to prevent himself from landing on his backside and dug into his pocket for the photograph and marker pen.

"Miss Tate?" he called. "Hannah? Could I have your autograph please? Hannah?"

"Get lost asshole," a fashionably unshaven monster hissed as he turned and glared at Santosh.

"Miss Tate?" he called again, much louder this time. "Hannah? Just an autograph please, I've been waiting three hours in the rain."

A face glared at him from the back seat of the Limo. A face he recognised. A face he adored. The face wasn't smiling.

"Look I'm sorry buddy. I'm tired and freezing cold and now I'm wet through. Maybe next time huh? Hey Buck, give the guy a photo or something will ya?"

"Sure thing Ma'am," a voice replied and a huge hand shoved a photo of Hannah at him.

Santosh watched as the limo sped away, the spray from the tyres splashing his jeans. The photo fluttered to the ground and began its roller coaster journey along the river in the gutter. Santosh walked back to the railway station with tears on his cheeks and as he sat on the train among the alcoholics and drug addicts, he realised with sadness that he was no longer a Hannah Tate fan. He felt heartbroken, almost like he felt when his favourite uncle had died, but this was different. His uncle hadn't snubbed him, hadn't called him an asshole and left him in the rain.

The next morning the sadness had been replaced by anger. He was not only angry at Hannah Tate and her brainless thugs who'd been so rude to him; he was angry at himself for giving her so much of his energy, time and emotion. He felt foolish and he didn't like being a fool. What he needed, he decided, was revenge to make him feel better and what better way to get revenge on someone well known, than to tell his story to the world so that all those other idiots who spent their money on her would know what she's really like. Even if just a few stopped being fans, he would feel he'd got justice. He smiled as he set off to work and realised that he knew the perfect way to get the justice he craved.

Santosh Kumar was a journalist and quite a successful one with a large following on his internet blog and he knew that many other journalists and media folk read his website. He was a wordsmith by trade and although not quite the satirist that Dick Hanson was, he was good at his job. He was grinning all day as he thought about how to approach that night's blog and several times his buddies asked him what he was grinning about. Should he go for a scathing but humorous approach or just go in for the straight attack? By the time he shut his front door behind him that evening, he'd decided on a blend of the two. He'd use sarcastic humour alongside an honest, no nonsense attack on her attitude to the fans who pay for her privileged lifestyle. He would tell his story factually, but readers would be left in no doubt as to how badly he'd been treated. He stayed up until three in the morning finishing his blog entry and by the time he sat back to re-read it, he was pleased. He'd used just enough sarcasm to mock her ability without sounding petulant, whilst explaining the shameful way she and her minders had treated him. He questioned her motives, her morals and her abilities, he dug into her background and hinted, without actually saying so, that it looked like she was once a prostitute who got her first break by sleeping with a record producer who had tried to sell his story to a tabloid. He then finished it off by praising a new rising star of the jazzy ballad song, a direct competitor to Hannah Tate, and espousing her wonderful pure voice, her beauty and her dedication to her art.

The next day was Saturday so he slept in and awoke to sunshine and blue skies and felt happy. He spent the morning packing up all of his Hannah Tate CD's to give to a charity shop collection. It was a liberating experience for him and after enjoying a healthy tuna salad lunch, he opened his web page to see how his blog had been received. He was amazed to see over a hundred comments in less than the twelve hours it had been up and there was quite a debate going on between the die hard fans and those who had shared similar experiences to Santosh's. A broad grin split his face when he realised his side of the debate was clearly winning. By the next afternoon, his blog had gone viral all over the popular social networking sites and Hannah Tate's treatment of her fans was the hot topic of the day. Santosh whooped with glee and opened a bottle of wine to celebrate.

Two weeks later the first letter arrived. Santosh opened it, assuming it was a flyer from some charity asking for a donation but the breath left him as he read the cut out newspaper letters that spelled out the single word that filled the centre of the page.

'ASSHOLE.'

After the initial shock had worn off, he was annoyed and scanned it into his computer and uploaded it to his web page to fuel the still ongoing Hannah Tate, love her or hate her debate. It was followed by another, three days later and they continued twice weekly. All were made from cut out newspaper letters and all were similar in tone. Name calling, swearing and general hate filled spewings and he began to wonder whether he should call the police or not. After the first couple, he started to recognise the phrases and frequent mispellings and decided to try to preserve them as evidence. He was a fan of police forensic TV shows and reckoned he knew how to deal with them without contaminating them with his own fingerprints or DNA. He bought a box of latex gloves, freezer bags and parcel tape and carefully bagged and tagged each one with the date of arrival before storing them in a lidded box in his attic. Six weeks after that first letter, the first package arrived and as he looked down at the now familiar hand writing, he went cold.

Carefully feeling around all sides of the shoe box sized package, he finally decided he couldn't feel any wires or unusual lumps that might indicate a device of some kind, so he donned his latex gloves and carefully slit open the brown paper wrapping. Inside was indeed a shoe box so he used his pen knife to make a small slit in one side. With the aid of a torch, he peered inside to find what looked like a plastic bag, but thankfully no wires. With a steady hand, he extended the slit across and down on two sides and gently pulled down the flap. Inside was a large plastic bag containing a huge turd. More packages arrived, one a week alongside the letters, and contained various kinds of animal droppings, dead birds and other small creatures. After three months he received one containing a carefully dissected rat with its insides spread out and pinned to a board. Newspaper letters were stuck to one of the long sides and spelled out a chilling message.

'THIS WILL BE YOU SOON.'

This was the first direct threat and he became scared. He changed the locks and installed a bright security light above his front door and took to setting up his video camera in his hallway each night when he went to bed. The letters and packages continued and after a while he became less afraid. Nothing had happened to him out of the ordinary and he guessed that whoever it was that was doing it, was just out to scare him.

And so it was that he found himself drinking his reheated coffee and deciding not to go and see Hannah Tate in concert the following week. Besides, that day was his birthday and a few of his work buddies were taking him out for a drink and a meal before spending the night at his house with beer and bad movies to inspire column inches for their respective newspaper columns and web pages. He spent the next week looking forward to his birthday night out and even the letters and package didn't spoil his mood.

The last thing he remembered was being helped to bed by Phil and Josh before passing out. The combination of cider, tequila shots and a very hot curry, followed by more cider and two bad movies at home with the guys, all ensured he would be hung over for the next two days straight. He awoke thirsty, his head swimming and decided he should at least try to stagger through to the kitchen for some water otherwise he'd never get back to sleep again. He tried to sit up but couldn't, his hands were somehow stuck and try as he might, he couldn't free them. He swore revenge on his buddies for this stupid party trick but realised he'd probably have done the same to them, and would do at the earliest opportunity.

"He's awake." Santosh heard the voice from the corner of his bedroom and turned to see who had spoken but it was too dark to make out who it was.

"Phil? Josh? C'mon guys let me up. I need a drink. Come on this isn't funny and you know I'll get revenge when it's your birthday."

"Hello there Santosh," a woman's voice purred at him in the darkness.

"Who is that?" he called. He couldn't remember inviting any women back home. Maybe the guys had bought a prostitute for him. He hoped she was at least reasonable looking and not some huge ugly granny-gram or something. "What's going on?"

"You wanted my attention honey, well now you have it. Or rather, I have yours," she purred.

"What the fuck?" he replied as he heard footsteps approach. "Will you just let me up so I can get a drink of water? Did the guys pay you to do this? Whatever they paid you, I'll double it if you just let me up okay?"

"Oh you're not going anywhere my friend," the voice said. Suddenly the bedside light flicked on and Santosh gasped as he found himself staring into the face of Hannah Tate, famous jazzy ballad singer who had played in town that very evening.

82

Delectus Morbidium

He gasped in shock. "Hannah Tate? What are you doing here in my house and why am I tied up?"

"Now that's no way to welcome an international superstar. You should be more polite."

Santosh became angry. "Polite? Are you serious lady? Don't make me laugh."

"Oh I'm deadly serious honey," she replied as she threw one leg over the bed and sat astride him. "With the accent on deadly." She then laughed, a loud cackle that reminded Santosh of the wicked witch of the north from the Wizard of Oz.

"You crazy bitch," he spat, a mixture of anger and fear coursing through his body. "Get the fuck out of my house."

"Oh I will, don't you worry, but not before I've had some fun. Come now, haven't you dreamed of having Hannah Tate in your bed?"

"Not since you ditched me in the rain without so much as an autograph, no. Those thugs of yours called me an asshole if I remember correctly, before shoving me to the ground. Is that the way to treat people who've bought you your mansion, limo and jewellery huh?"

"Oh come on honey, it was raining. You wouldn't have wanted me to get all wet and freezing cold after singing for two hours would you?"

"Why not? I spent three hours out there in the freezing rain waiting for you. A couple of minutes and a damp hairdo wouldn't have killed you."

"So just because you didn't get a photo and an autograph, you have to try and ruin my career huh?" The fake smile fell from her lips and was replaced by a sneer. That blog of yours cost me seven dates on a concert tour and my perfume line was withdrawn from several websites."

"Oh what a shame," Santosh sneered back. "I guess you'll have to cancel the three month vacation in the Maldives this year. Poor you."

She slapped him across the jaw so hard it made his eyes water. He tried to kick out but found his ankles were also bound.

"Poor me? Oh no, you've got it all wrong honey. You see I'm gonna come out of this the heroine and everyone is gonna love me for what I do in your memory."

"In my memory? What the fuck are you talking about?"

"After I kill you, the world is going to know of the brave Hannah Tate fan who was so upset at not getting an autograph that he posted a scathing blog about her. Even when he was cruelly murdered by an intruder, Hannah Tate doesn't hold his attack on her against him. No, she does a concert tour in his name and donates half the proceeds to charity. The Santosh Kumar memorial tour. That's got a ring to it, don't you think?"

"You're going to kill me because of my blog? That's crazy."

"That's the last time you call me crazy, asshole," she spat as she reached behind her and brought out a long dagger. Santosh went cold to the bone, his eyes widening in fear as the knife approached him. He felt the cold metal against his adam's apple and swallowed involuntarily.

"Please don't," he begged. "I'll post a retraction, say I'm sorry. Whatever you want me to say. Please."

The rest of the sentence was cut off as the dagger sliced through his vocal chords. Santosh was just aware of something hard slicing through his throat and coming to rest against his cervical vertebrae, before he passed out.

"Bye bye honey." She smiled and began to sing as she sliced. The song so beloved of her fans filled the small bedroom and she decided to rename it in honour of Santosh, her fan who had been so cruelly murdered.

THE END

TEMPUS FUGIT
starring Steve Pannel, Sood Saab & Omar Al Farsi

Professor Pannel looked up from his notes, irritated by the intrusion of Malkin, his efficient but humourless butler.

"Yes Malkin, what is it?"

"Forgive the intrusion Professor Pannel. I know you said specifically that you weren't to be disturbed until nine but Doctors Saab and Al Farsi are both here and demanding to see you."

The professor sighed deeply and banged a fist on the table. "Okay, show them into the sitting room and offer them a drink would you? I'll be there in five minutes."

"Yes Sir," Malkin replied, giving a slight nod.

"Well good evening Steve," Doctor Omar Al Farsi grinned as the Professor entered the sitting room. "We were beginning to wonder if you didn't like our company any more, weren't we Sood."

Doctor Saab nodded. "Indeed we were. We haven't seen you in two weeks Steve, what's going on?"

"Yes come on," Omar continued. "What new secrets have you stumbled upon that you don't want to share with your two best friends?"

"Maybe it's a woman?" Sood grinned and Omar nodded.

"Or maybe a man."

"Oh stop it you two," Professor Pannel cut in before the tone could be lowered even further.

"Then what has turned you into such a recluse?" Sood asked with a grin.

"I'm just busy that's all."

"Busy with what?" Omar enquired.

"Just research," the Professor hedged.

"Just research huh?" Omar said as he cast a sideways glance at Sood and winked. "What are you researching? How to understand the complexities of the female mind perhaps?"

"Or a cure for alcohol induced impotence?" Sood offered and both men laughed heartily.

The Professor grinned along with them. Omar and Sood had been his best friends since their first days at university and throughout the intervening years, they had worked and played as a team. Being friends with these two had paid unexpected dividends when they were young and lusty. Women were always drawn to his two friends' exotic looks and he seldom failed to pick up a willing companion from amongst the crowd. They had spent hours arguing science theories back and forth across their different disciplines and never once lost respect for each other. Doctor Omar Al Farsi was an astro physicist, Doctor Sood Saab, a quantum physicist whilst Professor Steven Pannel had chosen Temporal Mechanics as his path.

He'd been fascinated by time since he was a young boy and had read The Time Machine by H G Wells. He still had the same dog eared hardback all these years later and couldn't imagine parting with it for anything. As he progressed through his education, he quickly gained a reputation as someone with a somewhat less than ordinary view on his chosen subject. He was firmly convinced that time could be manipulated enough to allow a person to travel back and forth in time and had enjoyed many a debate on the various theories, both for and against, with his two best friends.

"I've been wrestling with the last few equations that have so far prevented me from moving forward."

"Equations?" Sood asked, immediately interested. "Well if it's equations that are bothering you then I'm your man. Quantum physics is full of them."

"Hey I'm not exactly a stranger to them myself you know," Omar said with a grin. "Astro physics is just a pseudonym for 'far too many bloody equations.' It sounds better, rolls off the tongue easier and looks nicer on your resume."

"What sort of equations are you wrestling with anyway?" Sood asked as he helped himself to another drink.

"Oh I'm not wrestling any more. I finally sorted through them during lunch. I was just taking a bite out of one of Malkin's delicious steak sandwiches when everything suddenly fell into place. Now I can finally move forwards with the project. I'm so relieved, I've been battling with those equations for the last fortnight."

"Well that's good news indeed," Omar said as he raised his glass. "Here's to steak sandwiches."

"Steak Sandwiches," Sood repeated, his glass held aloft. "So what's this mysterious project you're so excited about?"

"Excited and damn secretive," Omar replied. "Come on Steve, out with it."

"It was the distortions you see," Professor Pannel explained. "I couldn't work out how to stop the temporal distortions that kept shutting it down."

"Shutting what down?" Sood asked.

"The wormhole," the Professor replied. "There were just too many distortions to allow the wormhole to become traversable and no matter how I tried, I couldn't figure it out until that steak sandwich. It's magnets. After all this time, the solution was magnetism. So simple and straightforward. Oh the relief is indescribable."

"Wormholes?" Omar exclaimed in shock. As an astro physicist, wormholes were his territory and he knew they were still little more than theory. A theoretical way of travelling huge distances across the gulf of space in seconds, wormholes were an accepted theory but nothing more than that. In the movies, wormholes had been happily sending people across galaxies for years but Omar firmly believed they would never actually be proved. He was also aware of the theory of wormholes being a method of time travel and guessed that it was this aspect that interested Professor Pannel.

"Even if we could prove the potential for a wormhole, accepted theory tells us they cannot ever actually be traversable." Omar was in his element, debating his favourite subject with one of his best friends.

"The quantum effects would never allow it," Sood added. "We've had this discussion before Steve. Even though general relativity does allow for the possibility of time travel, you'd have to exceed the speed of light to achieve it."

"I can assure you both that wormholes can be produced easily and the distortions that prevent them being traversable, caused by those quantum effects you're so fond of Sood, are easily dealt with by the proper use of magnetism and enough power."

"Oh come on Steve," Omar laughed. "I know you're passionate about time travel but to say you can assure us that you can create a traversable wormhole is preposterous."

"Preposterous eh?" Professor Pannel grinned. "Come with me gentlemen." He turned and walked towards the door. Down the hall, he dug into his pocket and extracted a large key, which he used to open the door to the basement of his large detached residence, left to him by his late father. With practiced ease he reached up and caught the dangling cord and pulled, flooding the stairway with light and the three descended.

"What you are about to see has never been seen by anyone other than myself, and you must both give me your solemn word that news of what you are about to see will never be passed to another living soul without my prior consent. This is not negotiable and if you cannot, then you are free to leave now."

"Oh you have my word," Omar announced, hand on his chest. "On my honour."

"And mine," Sood nodded. "My lips are sealed."

Professor Pannel nodded, a smile just visible on his lips. He was delighted to be able to share this at last with his two best friends and who knows, maybe soon the three of them would be exploring time together like those brave adventurers in all those movies they'd seen. He opened the door and reached for a switch on the wall. The

88

basement was flooded with light and the three looked at the imposing structure at the far end.

circular platform, approximately three feet in diameter lay on the floor near the far wall of the room with what looked rather like a small lectern attached to the rear, on which was a console with an array of buttons, switches and readout screens. From either side of the platform rose metal posts that met overhead, both sporting what looked like nozzles equally spaced along their length

"What the heck is that?" Omar asked.

"That is my time distortion device," the Professor explained. Both men looked at him in shock, their eyes wide with disbelief. He smiled. "It creates a stable and traversable wormhole through which one can move either backwards or forwards in time."

"But that's crazy," Sood exclaimed, unable to take his eyes off the device. "Time travel is no more than theory."

"It is theory no more my friend," the Professor replied.

"You've tried it?" Omar asked.

"Not yet no. As I told you, I've been wrestling with the last equations and the solution only came to me today. Until now I've been unable to stabilise the wormhole itself, but with a few changes to the magnetism and power level, it should be ready in a few minutes." He wandered over to the device and began flipping switches and turning dials. Picking up a hand held transmitter, he returned to where his friends were still gaping in awe. With a last look at his friends' astonished faces, he flipped a switch on the transmitter.

The lights dimmed and all three looked up at the ceiling.

"What's happening?" asked Sood.

"Don't worry," the Professor explained, "it's just the power drain. The device needs a lot of power and it's safe to assume that everyone for several miles around will be wondering why their lights have dimmed. Can you hear that hum?" The friends nodded. "That's the wormhole being created. In a few seconds you'll see it. It's beautiful."

Gradually the hum rose in pitch until it was beyond the level their ears could detect. Twenty seconds later a swirling mist began to appear in the centre of the device, between the two upright metal posts. The mist continued to grow in both size and solidity until it looked like a swirling mini galaxy right here in the basement. The device itself had disappeared at the same moment the wormhole gained its optimum size and stability and the three stood there speechless as they gazed at its swirling beauty.

"That's amazing," Omar whispered. "You did it. You actually did it. You old dog. I take back everything I said."

"It's beautiful," Sood added. "The most beautiful thing I ever saw."

"How can you control how far back or forwards it will take you?" Omar asked, suddenly very interested in how this thing worked.

"It's all in the wavelength," the Professor replied. "Adjusting the wavelength, longer or shorter, determines how far back or forwards I go."

"And how do you control whether you go back or forwards?"

"That's dependent upon how much I distort the fabric of space-time itself and in which direction I distort it. If I distort it in one direction, I go back in time and if I distort it in the opposite direction, I should go forwards."

"And how do you intend to return?" Sood asked. "If you go back to a time before the device was created, how can you use it to return? Surely it will remain here, in this moment in time?"

"That was a puzzle for quite a while," the Professor smiled. "I had to reconfigure the device so that when the wormhole is created, it completely envelops the whole device, effectively sending it through time first. I then follow it and emerge in a different time, in this same spot. The wormhole itself begins here and its other end, the destination end if you like, is also here but in another moment of time. Unlike the kind of wormhole you'd need to traverse across space, this one is designed specifically to distort only time. When I wish to return, I simply use the device in the same way, reversing the distortion flow of course, to move either backwards or forwards in time, back to here in this moment."

"But the dangers," Omar began. "You can't honestly say you're going to try it?"

"I am indeed going to try it," the Professor replied. "I'm going to go back in time one hour and when you arrive at this house, I shall quote a poem to you. When I return to this time again, you can repeat the poem to me and that will be your proof."

"But it won't work," Sood exclaimed. "It can't work. Don't you see? If it were possible to go back in time and do as you say, Omar and I would already know the poem. It would have happened in our past, one hour ago. The fact that neither of us remembers you quoting any poem to us proves that you didn't travel back in time."

"He's right Steve," Omar nodded. "This is just too dangerous. You can't do this now, not without further testing. Let's wait and get the top guys in the field onto it. Now you've proven that a wormhole can be created, we'll have something to study. This will get you a Nobel Prize or I'll eat his hat," he nodded towards Sood.

"Now you're just being pussies," the Professor countered. "However long we wait, someone has to step into that wormhole sometime. We can only study for so long before we need to get off our asses and give it a try. Don't worry, I've got no family and neither am I encumbered by debt. I've made my last will and testament and have left everything to the Temporal Studies Institute."

"Steve, please, don't do this," Sood said as he put a hand on his friend's shoulder.

"I have to," the Professor replied. "I've been waiting for this moment all of my life." He stepped towards the still whirling light.

"Steve, you can't do this," Omar called, "not yet. Please wait a while."

"I'll be back before you know I've gone."

The first thing he was aware of was a momentary burst of intense cold that chilled him through to the marrow. He felt his body explode;

each cell detached itself from its neighbours and expanded outwards. There was no pain, just this weird exploding expansion and for a moment, he was acutely aware of each single cell that made up his whole body. His awareness of one cell was no greater nor less than his awareness of each of the others, all at the same time and all separate from one another. Then, all at once, everything reversed and his cells recombined with a bone crushing heaviness that took his breath away. He felt heavy, awkward and all about him was darkness. He could see nothing and feel nothing. There was nothing beneath his feet and he couldn't tell if he was upside down or the right way up. Everything was a black void.

"Hello," he called into the void. "Is anyone here?" He became frightened as the words of his friends came flooding into his mind. Over the years of their friendship they'd argued the subject of time travel many times and both Omar and Sood were of the opinion that it couldn't happen. They'd argued that time was simply the now, this moment in which we exist now and once gone, that moment ceases to be as we move into a new moment of now. The past therefore, they'd argued, simply didn't exist and neither could the future as we hadn't yet reached that moment of now.

"Oh my God," he cried out into the void. "I was so wrong. Help me, someone please." Professor Steven Pannel floated through the void and screamed into the darkness while back in the now, Doctor Omar Al Farsi and Doctor Sood Saab worried for their friend. For long hours into the night they sat vigil in the deserted basement, hoping and praying he would return to them. He never did of course, for he had travelled to a moment that was outside of time, a memory that no longer existed in any temporal sense, and when one is trapped outside of time, one cannot return to it.

He floated through the void, time of no meaning or value to him. Unable to be influenced by the passing of time, Professor Pannel did not age, his body did not wither, nor did his mind falter. He remained, alone and afraid in the dark in a place outside of time, and will remain so until the concept of time itself is but a distant memory.

THE END

TENNER AN HOUR
starring Sherry Smith & Diane Lira

Diane sipped her tea and smiled to herself in triumph. She could not remember being able to enjoy the simple pleasure of a quiet cuppa without interruption for years. If he wasn't demanding his breakfast he was demanding the newspaper. If it wasn't the newspaper then he needed cigarettes from the corner shop. If it wasn't cigarettes then he was moaning that the house was untidy. All he ever did was moan about everything. She wondered why she put up with it for so long. She wished she listened to her mother but back then, she was a headstrong girl and the very fact her mother didn't like him was guaranteed to make her stay with him just to spite her. She looked around her and realised that yes, the place was a little untidy and could do with a spring clean. She might even get a painter in to redecorate now that Henry was gone. There was a little money put by that she managed to save from his pension without him knowing and there was still a bit of her Uncle's legacy left.

When she finished her tea she rummaged under the sink for some bin bags and trudged upstairs to the bedroom she shared with Henry for a loveless forty years of wedded bliss. She laughed at the expression.

"Wedded bliss? With Henry?" she laughed out loud, "can't remember the last time he got romantic." She spent the next couple of hours filling five of the bin bags with all of Henry's clothes before dragging them downstairs and leaving them by the side of the dustbin. She put aside his mother of pearl cufflinks and his wedding ring and bagged a few other things up for the charity shop.

"Might get a few pounds for these," she muttered to herself, "thanks old man."

She opened the window and sniffed.

"Phew, it's getting a bit ripe in here, dirty old bugger," she cursed and decided to employ a cleaner once a fortnight to keep the place up together now she was on her own.

The bus lurched to a stop and splashed freezing dirty water over Diane's ankles. She glared at the driver as she showed her bus pass and went to find a seat. As usual, all the front seats were occupied by teenagers with those things in their ears that made an annoying noise. Opposite was a girl with a baby that screamed its head off the whole way into town and by the time the bus approached her stop, her ears were ringing and she was wishing she could wring its neck without being noticed. She lumbered off the bus without thanking the driver; her ankles were still wet and cold, and trudged up the hill to the pawn shop. Once inside she handed over Henry's cufflinks and wedding ring and waited for the funny little man with the wispy ginger beard to rip her off.

"I'll give yer twenty quid for the lot," he offered.

"Thirty," she countered.

"Twenty five and that's my final offer," he said and she nodded.

"Oh go on then. Forty years of marriage and what am I left with? Twenty five quid. Thanks Henry you miserable git."

She pocketed the money and went to leave but then noticed some cards in the window and stopped to read them. One was from a girl offering to do cleaning.

"Tenner an hour eh?" she muttered to herself, "not bad that. I'll give her a ring when I get home." She jotted down the number and began the trudge back to the bus stop and hoped the return journey would be free of screaming babies. It wasn't!

The doorbell rang smartly at ten o clock and Diane went to answer it. A young woman stood on the doorstep, smiling and nervous.

"Err hello, Mrs Lira? I'm Sherry and I've come to clean for you."

"Do come in dear, it's a bit untidy I'm afraid. My late husband was a messy old sod and now that he's gone I'd like it clean again like it used to be."

"Not a problem Mrs Lira. Now where would you like me to start?"

"Oh anywhere you like dear, the whole place needs a good do."

"Okay well shall I start upstairs then and work my way down?"

"Yes that'd be lovely dear."

Diane heard Sherry stomping up the stairs and along the landing, whistling a tune to herself. She was going to enjoy having a cleaner coming every fortnight. Someone to natter to and get the place clean again.

The scream startled Diane and made her drop the soapy teacup. It fell to the floor and broke clean in half. She put down the tea towel and trundled through to the hall and called up the stairs.

"Whatever is the matter dear?"

No answer came back, the screaming cleaning girl was oblivious to Diane's enquiries so she started up the stairs. She entered the bedroom to find the girl standing at the end of the bed, hands up to her face still screaming her head off. She suddenly looked at Diane and muttered something unintelligible before running out of the room. Diane heard her thudding down the stairs and then the clatter of the door as it banged against the wall. She could hear the girl screaming as she ran right down the street and into Waverley Place.

"What on earth got into her then Henry?" Diane said as she turned and looked at the bed. The corpse was now beginning to smell and opening the window each day wasn't doing much good anymore.

"I'm going to have to find a new cleaner now. This is all your fault you old sod," she raged at the lifeless body, the axe still buried within the skull. "Look at this place, if it weren't for you being so damn lazy it'd be nice and clean, now look at it," she said in disgust as she looked at him. The blood had soaked right through the bed and onto the carpet; the congealed mass now a writhing mass of maggots. She sighed and trudged back down the stairs and put the kettle on.

"Think I'll have a nice cuppa."

THE END

97

THE HIKER

How the fuck did I get into this situation? If I read this in a book or saw it in a movie I'd be the first to laugh and call it ridiculously implausible. Don't get me wrong, I have an imagination; I'm not some fixed, left brained nerd who can't see outside the box. It's just that this situation I'm in is so completely, out there, that even I can't believe it. At least I didn't believe it but now I'm beginning to realise that perhaps I might have to.

It was the cold that started it. Until it started to get cold here I managed to hold onto the belief that perhaps this was all an amazing day dream. I spent a few hours reliving all those scenes I've watched in all those science fiction movies, and tried to work out just exactly what the big hunky hero would do now. Trouble is, I don't happen to have the pen knife, ice pick or paper clip that could save the day. Why is it that the hero in a movie always just happens to have the right piece of equipment handy just when they need it?

It was such a beautiful morning when I got up today too but why couldn't I have just stayed home and done the laundry? What's wrong with laundry for fuck's sake? I suppose this is the moment when I wish I hadn't moved into this area at all and yeah, I admit I'm now thinking perhaps there wasn't so much wrong with New York after all. I know the rush and the noise and the fumes get on everyone's nerves but y'know what? You get used to it. Everything you could need is right on your doorstep and there's even Central Park if you want rural anytime. But no, I had to do something stupid and move to the country.

If only it wasn't so cold and it's getting dark now too. I'm glad I had the presence of mind to at least bring a weatherproof jacket with me, despite the sun. Why the fuck did I uproot myself from my good job and nice apartment just for the sake of a few trees? Granted, this forest is beautiful but there are trees in Central Park, why weren't they enough for me? Why am I never satisfied and why do I always have to go to extremes and why did I end up like this? And more to the point, why the fuck doesn't anyone else ever walk around here?

If I had just stayed home and maybe gone to the store or something, I might've met that cute guy who works in the coffee shop; the one with the mysterious eyes who smiled shyly at me as he handed me my tuna sandwich and coffee. He might even have summoned up the nerve to ask me out to a movie or maybe a meal at that new Mexican place. Instead I'm here, cold, damp and scared cos it's getting dark and I don't want to cry like a stupid girl, even though I am a stupid girl.

I'm that person all those infomercials warn you about; the one you could be if you don't heed their advice or buy their product. Boy do I wish I'd paid attention now. Why I ever thought a fifty five function Swiss pocket knife was a waste of money I'll never know, I mean why would anyone leave the house without one? People should be made to carry them by law. I promise to buy one when I get home, I promise okay? Now for fuck's sake get me out of here please.

I don't even like hiking really. I only do it because it's an easy way to keep in shape and see the countryside. My mom always said that the best men like to walk in nature because it shows they have a good attitude, and that I should learn to love it too so that I could attract the right sort of husband. Damn you mom! No guys hike out here, no one hikes out here; I've been here all day and haven't seen a soul okay? I'm sorry mom, I didn't mean to yell but it's cold and dark and I'm scared and I'm hungry. Hang on a minute, don't I still have a Hershey bar left? Let me just see if I can dig in my pocket, oh yeah here we go. A bit bashed about but hey, it's a Hershey bar. Oh my god that tastes like heaven. Normally I'm careful with chocolate but I think I can relax my rules a little; this situation calls for a slightly different set of priorities and I'm not going to worry about one little Hershey bar. If necessary I'll do an extra yoga class or two when I get out of this stupid situation.

You know what? When you live in the city you think night time is dark but you have no idea what dark is until you come out here. It is so dark here now, like nothing you can imagine and the noises? The noises are creeping me out like you wouldn't believe. We all know critters live in the forest, even I know that but somehow these noises don't sound like they come from something cute and fluffy. These noises sound like teeth and claws and, oh shit there it goes again; a growl, bark and shriek all rolled into one. Holy mamma I've never been so scared in all my life and I wanna go home. Maybe if I try and go to sleep it will just go away.

What the fuck? Oh wow at least it's morning; no more dark for at least twelve hours and maybe today's the day the newly formed handsome guy hiking club will find its way here. There's always hope huh? You know I had this weird dream. There was this huge, hey what was that? I'm sure I heard a noise. It sounded like an engine backfiring but it can't be. There can't be anything with an engine out here that's just, there it is again and yeah it's an engine and where there's engines there's people, oh thank heavens. Yep it's definitely engines, and more than one of them by the sound of it.

Well I've been hearing the engines for, oh I dunno, a couple of hours and they're real close now and I think I heard voices too. Hey look over there, if I crane my neck right round I can see a flash of yellow and there's guys with chainsaws, wow that blonde is a hunk. Maybe it's worth yelling now they're close.

"Help. Hey guys, I'm over here. Help me please. Guys. Hey over there, help me please. Please guys, I'm hurt and can't get up and I've been out here all night. Help."

Oh thank god, I think he heard me. He's looking this way anyhow. Oh, yeah he's seen my frantic waving, oh thank god. Man he's even more gorgeous up close, but he sure don't look too well. He must've eaten something that disagreed with him. How embarrassing for the guy to bring up his guts just as he rescues a cute damsel in distress. Hey don't leave, come back. You can't leave me here. Hey.

"What's your problem Greg?"

"Over there Sir, you better come see for yourself."

"Okay okay let's have a look at what scared ya. You're such a pussy at times. Holy mother of god. Oh shit. Oh fuck me."

"Pussy Sir?"

"Call the cops for Christ's sake Greg. Someone call the damn cops."

"How long do you reckon it's been here Sir?"

"I've no idea. Years though probably."

"What do you think happened?"

"I've no idea. Hang on though, what's that? Looks like one of the leg bones is broken and look at those scratches on the side of the skull."

"Yeah I see em. What do ya suppose made those?"

"Well years ago, before this area got built up, this was a huge forest and there was Grizzlies here. Maybe this person has been here since those days and got caught by one. Who knows."

"One thing's for sure Sir. This'll hold up the building for a while."

"Yep, it sure will. Damn."

THE END

THE LAST MAN

Oh hi buddy, I was beginning to think I'm the only man on Earth. Man am I glad to see you. You know all those times you say to someone, "if I was the only man on earth I wouldn't want to fuck her?" Well I'm that guy and I can tell you that I would love to fuck her. After being alone on this god forsaken world for just over three months now I can say with complete authority that yes, I would indeed fuck her.

So how did it happen? I suppose that's the first thing I ought to explain. I mean, you can't just tell someone you're the only man on Earth without explaining why you're saying it, can you? The trouble is I can't explain it. I don't know how it happened, nor why; all I know is that it did and here I am. The other odd thing; I mean apart from being the only man on Earth, which is pretty weird you have to admit, is that I really am the only man on Earth. What I mean is, there aren't any bodies or anything; no rotting corpses stinking up the place and going squidgy everywhere and no skeletons sitting in Beemers at traffic lights. Nothing, nada, zip.

Everything was fine the day it happened. The thirty first of August was a work day so I got up at seven as I always do during the week. I had my shower, brushed my teeth, ate my cereal, drank my coffee and kissed my wife before setting out to walk the quarter mile to the railway station. I remember the train was ten minutes late and I was annoyed because I was desperate to take a piss and as the train is usually bang on time, it means I don't normally have time to do it until I get on the train. If I take the time to go to the railway station bathroom, I run a serious risk of missing the train, so I always hang on. That day I hung on and the train was late and I was very uncomfortable by the time it arrived. It was actually as I was taking that much needed piss when it, whatever it was, happened. I remember going to the bathroom on the train, closing the door behind me and unzipping. I'd just started to pee when I remember hearing a high pitched whine from somewhere. It was quiet at first and I ignored it but it quickly grew louder and became so obvious that I had to take notice.

The next thing I remember is standing in the middle of the road outside my own house and wondering how I'd got there and why I'd come back there when all I'd wanted was to take a piss. I looked down at myself and found I still had my zipper undone, so I did myself back up and went indoors to think about what the heck had happened to me. I called out to Becky, my wife, but she'd obviously gone out as the place was silent. Only she hadn't gone out at all; she'd just gone but I didn't know that then. I looked at the clock and it said nine minutes past nine, which was the next weird thing as at that time I was on the train taking a piss, the piss. Then I noticed the clock had stopped working altogether so I had no clue what time it was now. I looked at my wrist watch and it said nine minutes past nine. What the fuck?

By now I was thinking maybe I'd had some sort of breakdown or panic attack or fit or something, and I was getting seriously freaked out by the notion that I might be losing my mind at fifty years old. Life was pretty stressful of course, it is for everyone these days but I didn't think it so stressful that I'd go crazy just like that while taking a piss on a train.

What's that you say? Go with you? Well umm okay I guess it can't do any harm now anyway.

I sat and chilled all day and just tried to relax, and it wasn't until it was long past the time when my wife should've come home that I got seriously worried. I tried to call her cell phone but the line was dead so I went out into the street and watched for her for at least a half hour before I got the first inkling that there was more going on here than just me having a funny turn while taking a piss. You see, we live on a busy road and there's always traffic going up and down night and day. We can't yet afford to move into somewhere a bit more secluded, y'know with our own garden back and front and maybe even a driveway or a garage to put the car. We both pay the mortgage on our apartment and it's expensive even with two wages coming in. Anyway, that's what it was you see; there was no traffic for the whole half hour I was out there waiting for Becky. That's my wife by the way, you'd like her.

Once I realised that there hadn't been a single car, truck or motorcycle, I listened hard and y'know what? There wasn't even a bird or a bug making any noise at all. I went to the house next door to our apartment block and banged on the door but no one was at home. I tried three houses on our street and no one was at home at any of them and by this time I was like, what the fuck is going on here? I was panicking man.

What? Go in here? What do you want to go in here for? It's just a bone yard like any other. Cemeteries creep me out but hey, I'm just happy to have some company so if you want to visit here, that's fine by me buddy.

I must've wandered all night, knocking on doors and yelling through windows and by dawn I was so tired and panicking and lonely that I sat down in the middle of the street and cried. I don't mind admitting it to you, yeah I cried and I don't think any man would've done differently in the same position. After a few days I began to think that maybe they finally dropped the bomb or something, y'know, the terrorists? Then I realised that if they had dropped the bomb there'd be bodies everywhere and I'd be sick from radiation poisoning. I remember seeing a film on TV about that happening, so I knew about the radiation. I didn't feel sick and I still don't so I figured it probably wasn't the bomb.

My next thought was a little crazy and I'm almost embarrassed to tell you about it but I thought maybe aliens had taken everyone away. Yeah, I know, crazy huh? The thing is though buddy, when you're in a crazy situation and you don't know what's happened or why, you start to think all sorts of weird shit and it seemed plausible at the time. At first I didn't think it was weird that maybe aliens had come and taken everyone. Perhaps their species was dying and they wanted us to interbreed with so they wouldn't die out or something, or maybe they were trying to save us from something that's about to happen to the planet and because I was taking a piss, they didn't realise I was left behind. If that's the case then I know Becky will try to persuade them to come back for me; she wouldn't just go away and not tell me. We have a great marriage y'know, we're tight. If she can, she'll do something from wherever she is and get me picked up as soon as she can; I trust her.

What's that? Is this the one you're visiting? You want me to leave you alone for a minute? You want me to go look at the grave? Why? Well okay if that's what you want. Is this your wife or your, hey what the fuck kind of sick joke is this? Don't look at me like that; tell me what's going on here. I don't know who you are, I came all the way out here with you to keep you company and I even came into the bone yard because you wanted to and now you show me a grave with my own name on? There must be loads of guys with the same name as me; it's not unusual or anything. You're just trying to creep me out because you've gone nuts being alone for so long since the aliens took everyone away, well screw you buddy. There are millions of guys in the world, or at least there were millions of guys in the world called Ray. Look, I'll prove it to you, see the stone? Look at it; it says there look, in loving memory of Ray. Loving husband of, what the fuck? Loving husband of Becky? But what? I don't understand; please tell me what's going on. I was just taking a piss on the train, that's all. Now I'm standing here with some strange guy who's showing me the grave of a guy with my name who was married to a gal with my wife's name.

Y'know buddy, if I didn't know better I'd swear you were trying to convince me that it's not them that's gone, but me. Well y'know what? That's crazier than aliens and I was embarrassed to think maybe aliens took everyone and left me but you? You're far crazier than me. No, don't bother following me, I'm going home and don't want to see you again. Just leave me alone. I want to go home and go to sleep; I'm real tired and can't take this shit any more. Maybe if I just sit down here for a bit and relax a while and calm down, maybe even get forty winks. I'll wake up when the sun rises and you'll be gone, this whole crazy situation will be gone.

Delectus Morbidium

Oh hi buddy, I was beginning to think I'm the only man on Earth. Man am I glad to see you. You know all those times you say to someone, "if I was the only man on earth I wouldn't want to fuck her?" Well I'm that guy and I can tell you that I would love to fuck her. After being alone on this god forsaken world for just over three months now I can say with complete authority that yes, I would indeed fuck her.

So how did it happen? I suppose that's the first thing I ought to explain.

THE END

THE MIRROR
Starring Debb Levoie

I guess I could blame my best friend for what's happened to me, but that would be wrong. It's all my own fault really. It's my fault, not only for letting Sherry talk me into it, but for making the decision to explore its potential. It was exciting and new and I couldn't resist, just couldn't resist. What harm could it do to just take a peek? Trouble was, one little peek wasn't enough. I wanted another, and another, and then the inevitable happened, I got careless. Now I can't change it back and I'm stuck with the situation. A very bad situation.

Sherry and I were cruising through our neighbourhood when she noticed a sign for a garage sale outside the gates to Amesbridge Manor, the big spooky house on the outskirts of town. The old place had recently been bought by some rich folks from out of town, we'd read about it in the newspaper and we both agreed we would love to get a look inside the old place. It had been empty for thirty years or so, after the last of the Amesbridge family disappeared without a trace one night. He was apparently a reclusive old man who had never married or had any children to pass the place on to. Anyway, Sherry caught sight of the sign and started everything.

"Hey Debb, look, did you see that?" she squealed.

"What? I do have to look at the road sometimes y'know," I sighed.

"There's a garage sale at the Manor tomorrow, I just saw the sign outside the gates."

"No. You're shitting me," I shot her a look.

"Hun, I shit you not," she declared. "We're gonna go of course?"

"Of course," I grinned. "What time does it start?"

"Ten in the morning."

"I've always wondered what it's like in there. I can hardly believe we're finally going to see inside the old place."

"Didn't the old Amesbridge guy disappear?" Sherry said and I nodded.

"Apparently so, yeah. Went to bed one night and wasn't there in the morning."

"He probably ran off with some girl half his age," Sherry giggled.

"Or most likely the butler did it," I countered and we both laughed.

We rolled up to the gates of Amesbridge Manor just before ten, and I secretly thought we'd find it all locked up as per usual, but to my surprise, a guy in a suit was unlocking the gates and waving us in. Sure enough, there was the sign by the left of the gate, 'Garage Sale, 10am Sunday.'

"You weren't shitting me after all," I grinned at Sherry, who rolled her eyes and shook her head at me.

I followed the signs around to the rear of the house and parked up. The only other vehicles were a fleet of huge trucks, into which items of furniture and packing cases were being loaded. The new owners were obviously taking the best stuff for themselves and selling off the junk. That was no surprise, but I hoped we'd find something that was at least unique and interesting, if not valuable.

"Okay Sherry, here we go," I smiled. "Remember, whatever we buy has to fit in the car, so don't go mad okay?"

"Okay," she nodded.

We were shown in to a huge room, which we were told was once a grand ballroom, but was now a faded memory of its former grandeur. Cobwebs hung in festoons from the faded and torn window drapes, wallpaper hung flacid from the walls and the once beautiful parquet floor was pitted and scarred. It felt sad. Sad and lonely and spooky as hell. We both shivered involuntarily and looked at each other with raised eyebrows.

Delectus Morbidium

"Welcome ladies," a guy in what was obviously a very expensive tailor made suit smiled. "Welcome to Amesbridge Manor. Feel free to spend as long as you want and rummage around, everything in this room is for sale."

We smiled and made our way clockwise around the room. We poked into boxes and rummaged through shelves and tables and although everything was the finest quality, nothing took my fancy. I almost bought a beautiful music box with an intricate inlaid lid, until I discovered the music didn't work. I didn't know anyone who could fix it and I really didn't want a broken music box in my modern apartment, even if it was over a hundred years old. By the time we got halfway around the room, more people had arrived and Sherry had spent over a hundred on five items.

It was as we were picking our way through boxes in a dark corner that I saw it, and made the worst decision of my life. The mirror was leaning against the wall, a drape of faded wallpaper hanging down over one corner of the heavily carved ebony frame. It stood six feet high and three feet wide and would look fabulous in my apartment. I fell in love instantly and bought it on the spot for three hundred and twenty five. It was so easy and I did it so innocently. There was no feeling of dark foreboding inside to warn me, no crash of thunder or flickering lights to tell me this was an extremely bad idea. So often since then, I've wished there had been something, anything, a sign of some sort. Trouble is, I loved that mirror so much that even if there had been a sign of impending doom, I would probably have ignored it. To cut a long and boring story short, the mirror cleaned up beautifully and did look fabulous in my apartment. I placed it at the top of my stairs, an imposing but beautiful sight as you entered the front door or climbed the stairs to bed. I was happy with it and everyone who came by, agreed it was lovely.

For two months my life continued as normal until one night, during a thunderstorm, I found myself awake and unable to get back to sleep at two twenty three in the morning. I went downstairs and got myself a drink, before heading back upstairs to bed. As I approached the mirror, something caught my eye and made me stop mid stride and gaze into its depths. As I looked, the reflection of my apartment changed slightly and I caught my breath in shock. I stepped closer and looked again and sure enough, the reflection of my apartment seemed to be fading in and out, competing for dominance with what looked like an old fashioned library, complete with crackling fireplace.

I stepped back and blinked hard, shaking my head, before looking again. Sure enough, there was the scene just as before. A crackling fireplace, a leather armchair, a Christmas tree and dark windows showing that it was night outside there, just as it was here. I reached out to the mirror and felt the cold hardness of the glass begin to soften under my fingers. Snapping my hand back in fear, I examined my fingers but they were undamaged. Trying desperately to calm my thumping heart, I debated with myself for what seemed like several minutes, before my curiosity took over and I reached out again.

For a moment, the mirror was solid beneath my fingertips, just as it should be, and I was just wondering whether I had imagined it, when it again began to soften beneath my fingers. This time, I stole myself not to flinch in terror and I pushed just a little. To my horror and surprise, my fingers continued sinking into the surface of the glass until my whole hand was gone. It was weird because I could see my hand reflected in the mirror, but it was only on the other side, not this side. I was on this side of it, but my hand on the other side, in the mirror. I could feel the heat from the fire in the library, whose reflection was staring back at me.

I found out by experience that this happened every morning at precisely two twenty three and it was some time before I put the pieces together and realised that what I saw in the mirror was a direct reflection of the last dream I had when I woke up. For a while I just thought it was some random thing that decided what I would see, until I recognised a scene from my childhood and remembered the dream I'd just had. So this was how it worked huh? Whatever you are dreaming about at two twenty three in the morning, will be in the mirror. I began setting my alarm for two twenty three and after a couple of weeks of standing and looking at my hand waving at me from inside the mirror, I finally plucked up the courage to put my head through. I was dying to step through and experience it fully and I knew it was just a matter of time before I got the courage up to try it.

I spent many happy nights exploring my old childhood home, made love to a gorgeous dark haired man by moonlight, rode horses through flowering meadows and once, was chased by a vampire down a dark alley. I made a decision after that one, to only go through the mirror if my dreams had been good ones. I didn't realise then, that much of what we dream about is lost the moment we wake and it was only a matter of time before my luck ran out.

I awoke with my alarm at two twenty three and remembered having a lovely dream of a warm sunny beach, palm trees and lapping waves. This would be a perfect one to try, after all, what harm is there in such a calm dream? I dressed in my bikini, stuck a hat on my head and carried a bag containing sun cream, my camera and a large bottle of water. Taking a deep breath, I stared at the beautiful scene in the mirror and sighed. It looked like the typical paradise island, the kind of place my salary would never be able to afford to take me. Slinging the bag over my shoulder, I put both arms through the mirror, then my head and took in the scene. The salty air struck my nostrils, the sound of the waves lapping on the shore, the rustle of the palm trees in the breeze and the heat of the tropical sun hit my face. With a deep breath, I boldly stepped through and felt the sand between my toes.

I spent a wonderful few hours just lying on the sand, swimming in the ocean and enjoying the sun and quiet, and all the time the mirror stood sentinel on the sand, the reflection of my own apartment looking back at me. Just as I was thinking I should return, I felt something change in the air around me. A chill swirled around me and goose bumps rose up on my arms. I looked about and saw the palm trees whipping furiously back and forth, as if gripped by a hurricane. My relaxed mood quickly turned to fear and I raced towards the mirror and the safety of my apartment. I was halfway there when I heard the roar and froze on the spot as the ground trembled beneath my feet. The crack of branches and snapping of tree trunks caught my attention and I looked to my left, just in time to see the head of a huge dinosaur emerge from the tree line and look right at me.

Our eyes met and the remainder of my dream came back to me, the bit I had forgotten as the alarm clamoured its way through to my consciousness and yanked me upwards to waking reality. I remembered the huge meat eater coming at me from the trees and my terrified flight from it, its footsteps shaking the ground as it quickly caught me up. I remembered the falling palm tree that blocked my path and how I was just about to leap it when the alarm woke me and reality swept away the frightening imagery. I shook myself from the memory and forced my fear-frozen body to run. The ground shook as the creature bore down on me from behind, but I forced myself to concentrate on nothing but running towards the mirror and safety. As I was running, a thought crept its way into my mind and made me cry out in terror. What if the creature could go through the mirror too?

A sound from my left made me snap my head around, just in time to see the huge palm tree hit the sand with a thud, twenty feet ahead. I knew I would be able to leap it easily enough, I had been good at sports in school and had kept myself pretty much in shape since then. I race towards the fallen tree, the thundering footsteps and roaring of the titan getting ever closer behind me. Just as I leapt into the air to hurdle the fallen palm tree, the mirror on which I had fixed my gaze, vanished into thin air. It was in those last moments that it all made sense at last. The mirror was tied into my dreams and entering the mirror allowed me to experience those dreams. Trouble is, when the dream ends, so does the mirror's attachment to it. I had spent too long here in the dream and now, as I turned to see the monster closing the distance between us, I peed myself in fear and began to cry.

THE END

THE SECRET RECIPE
starring Amanda Heath and Fiona McVie

Amanda yawned and stretched herself. Buddy the cat leapt onto the bed and nuzzled her face with his wet nose, his loud purring ringing in her ear.

"Okay okay," she groaned, "I hear ya. C'mon let me up and I'll give you your breakfast." She threw back the bedcover and swung her legs onto the floor. The wood was cold under foot and she felt around for her slippers as Buddy leapt off and ran to the door where he stopped and mewed loudly.

"All right, for heaven's sake. I'm coming," she chided as she wriggled her toes into the comforting sheepskin and stood up. Buddy led the way and Amanda padded into the kitchen to feed him and put the coffee on. "There ya go," she smiled as she put the plate of foul smelling meat onto the floor and watched as he sniffed daintily at it before giving it a tentative lick. She laughed and tutted at him and headed back to the bathroom to shower. On the way she heard the click of the letter box and turned to see a single white envelope land on the mat. Her heart leapt inside her breast as she looked at it and wondered whether she should shower first or open it now and end the agony of waiting.

"Oh for fuck's sake," she said aloud as she strode purposefully towards the door and picked up the envelope. "Ms Amanda Heath," she read aloud and smiled to herself. She'd never been called Ms before and she didn't think she liked it much. It made her sound old and dried up and she didn't intend to become either of those for a long time yet. She ripped it open and spread out the single sheet and within thirty seconds she gave a whoop of glee that scared Buddy out of his wits and put him right off his breakfast. She danced back to the bathroom and sang loudly throughout her shower and didn't give a damn if the guy in the apartment below could hear her or not. She was happy.

It was just three months since she'd had to downsize after the death of her husband and move to Claireview with just a few sticks of furniture and the ever faithful Buddy. She'd been lucky enough to find the run down apartment at an affordable rent and began the mind numbing search for a job. She soon realised she would have to lower her expectations a little, so it was with little enthusiasm that she applied for the job of kitchen assistant at Claireview Heights Restaurant. She hadn't done much cooking except for feeding herself and her husband since they'd been married so she wasn't that hopeful of landing the job. When the letter arrived offering her the post she was both amazed and delighted, despite not being that keen on the job in the first place. It was a job and that meant money. She hoped to be able to save up and maybe even buy her own place within five years or so.

The first day of her new job arrived and she made sure she arrived ten minutes early. She needed this job so she wanted to make a good impression. She would be working under Bob Lanes, the Head Chef and would take her orders from him first and foremost, although Mrs McVie, the Restaurant Manager was in overall charge. Bob was nice enough, although Amanda noticed he was a little rusty when it came to conversation, and she soon realised she was wasting her time trying to become friends with him. She started by doing all the nasty jobs like washing up and mopping floors, fetching, carrying and emptying bins but she forced herself to smile her way through the days and smiled gratefully when she received her paychecks.

After a month or two she was allowed to help prepare vegetables and spent her days chopping, slicing and dicing and Bob even showed her how to slice and chop like all the celebrity chefs she'd seen on the tv. She even started cooking more for herself at home and hoped that soon he would allow her into Claireview Heights' most famous secret - The Claireview Pie. This gastronomic delight was the restaurant's most famous delicacy and a closely guarded secret known only to Mrs McVie and Rob. Although she was allowed to help prepare the vegetables and sometimes even the pastry for these legendary wonders, she was never allowed to know anything about the meat content. She didn't even know what kind of meat they contained, for the meat was always prepared and cooked overnight while the rest of the staff were away.

One morning she turned up to find Mrs McVie stressed out, pacing up and down and moaning.

"What's wrong Mrs McVie?" she asked. "Anything I can help with?"

"Oh Amanda, what are we to do?" the woman fretted. "Bob is off sick with the most awful flu and can't get out of his bed. He's likely to be off work for at least a week and we only have enough meat prepared for today's pies."

"Oh dear," Amanda replied, trying to sound concerned whilst seeing a marvellous opportunity for herself. "Well if there's anything I can do to help, you have only to ask. You know you can trust me not to blab to anyone. The Claireview secret will always be safe with me." She smiled and went off to her day's chores.

As she was putting on her coat to leave after a heavier than usual day, Mrs McVie approached her.

"Amanda? I've been thinking. You've been a good employee since you became part of our little family and although this is not something we would normally consider for someone so new to the staff, our current emergency requires me to make a radical decision. Therefore, I'm offering you the chance to help me tonight with the pies."

"Oh Mrs McVie, I'd be honoured," Amanda grinned.

"Now then, this is a serious matter Amanda. This may seem silly but our pies are famous and we don't want any of our competitors getting our secret and taking our customers or we'll all be losing our jobs. Claireview is a small town and it can't support too many restaurants. Our pies are our advantage over the competition, understand? You need to give your solemn promise that you will never breathe a word to anyone other than Bob and I about what you will witness tonight, okay?"

In a large mixing bowl, Mrs McVie showed Amanda the secret mix of herbs and spices that would give the meat its uniquely piquant taste. She spent hours boiling bones for stock, chopping fresh green stalks and leaves, grinding seed pods in the old pestle and mortar and everything was measured by the pinch or the handful.

"Now let's go get the meat," Mrs McVie said and retrieved an old blackened key from her pocket and led Amanda through the back door and down to an outbuilding at the end of the yard. "This is your last chance Amanda," she said. "Once through this door your lips must never reveal anything to anyone." Amanda nodded and watched as Mrs McVie fumbled with the key, which squeaked as it turned the ancient lock.

It wasn't until her eyes adjusted to the gloom that Amanda realised what she was seeing and when she did, her mind froze in shock. This was something out of her worst nightmare and for a few seconds, she didn't know how to react. Her hands instinctively went to her throat as she stood and looked at the single corpse that swung serenely on its hook. Both legs were missing, as was one arm and both buttocks and the torso and head that remained was obviously female.

"No, no," she hissed as she began to back towards the door and found her exit blocked by Mrs McVie.

"Come now my dear, don't be shy," Mrs McVie coaxed. "You didn't think we earned our reputation by using the same rubbish everyone else uses did you? Nothing tastes quite like human flesh and with the right herbs and spices, it is the most delicious thing you will ever eat. You've eaten our pies many times yourself and you've always said how wonderful they taste."

"You're mad," Amanda exclaimed. "You're all crazy."

"Oh Amanda," Mrs McVie sighed sadly, "and I thought you were the right one to take over from me when I retired. I'm disappointed in you my girl, very disappointed. I've wasted time and money training you and this is how you repay me?"

"Let me out," Amanda yelled as she made a grab for the door which opened and in walked Bob, looking as un-flu-like as Amanda had ever seen anyone look. He grinned as he walked towards her and she backed away in fright.

"You see Amanda," he coo'ed. "Human flesh is a wonderful taste but the most wonderful of all, the most exotic and piquant, is the female of the species. Every night I scour the neighbouring cities for prostitutes and drop outs. Those who will not be missed are the ones I choose for our speciality pies. Since you do not wish to become part of the business and share in the profits, then you will become part of the business in another way." He began to laugh and approached her, the huge cleaver raised high glinting in the light of the single bulb that swung from the ceiling.

Mrs McVie sighed as she fixed the small card to the window and went to empty the bins. Outside, a young woman sauntered along and stopped when she saw the card. "Oh" she muttered to herself. "They need a kitchen assistant here. I think I'll apply for the job."

THE END

THE TABLET OF SONDAL DAR
starring Loreen Smallwood

Let me see, when did the trouble start? I'm tempted to say it was when I took the job, but even if I had turned it down, the problem would still have occurred. It may not have happened that day, or that week, or even that year, but sooner or later, the shit would have hit the fan. It was a disaster waiting to happen, and it took a little three year old kid to flip the switch and turn a normal boring day just like all the others, into some other kind of crazy you could never imagine.

I've been in security all my working life and when the research lab that was my employment for six and a half years, was moved several thousand miles away, I decided not to relocate. It didn't take me long to secure a position at the Museum of Civilisation and Ancient Culture, and as the pay was slightly higher than I'd been used to, I was pleased. I passed the imposing building every day on the bus to work at the lab and never guessed I'd be working there one day. It also cut my commute by almost half, which was a very welcome bonus.

I did a rotating shift pattern of early days, late days and nights, five days on and two off. I'm quite a chatty person, so I tend to enjoy the day shifts more than the nights. That place is pretty spooky at night believe me, and even though I'm a big guy, the place gave me the shivers more than once in the middle of the night. There are skeletons and mummified remains in some rooms and the quiet of the night tends to add weight to the shadows that loom in the corners and corridors. Hell, give me the noisy crowds of the daytime over the spooky nights any day.

That day started just like any other. I had a laugh with the other security guys in the staff kitchen over scrambled eggs and toast, before heading out to my allotted patch on the third floor, Ancient Cultures from the Middle East. I strolled through Ancient Egypt, along the corridor to the Minoan Civilisation and the Babylonia Room, then along another corridor to The Hittite Kingdom, Assyrian Empire and Troy. That left one room where the stuff that nobody could fit into any of the other civilisations was displayed. This room was where the scientists and various clever people who worked at the museum, put the stuff they were still investigating and working on. Sometimes it isn't immediately obvious which ancient people made this relic or that statue, and until they knew for sure, it went in what the staff referred to as, the orphans room.

By mid morning there was quite a crowd. There was one school party of ten to twelve year olds who were, for the most part anyway, well behaved. A pretty blonde teacher accompanied them and she smiled at me as I strolled past. I smiled back and held in my gut until I was out of sight and then chastised myself for being an idiot. An old guy nodded to me and I nodded back; I recognised Professor Halpern as a regular visitor and laughed to myself as he peered over his glasses at a lump of rock with symbols scratched into the surface. That old guy visited the museum at least twice every week and always spent the entire time on the third floor, peering silently at the displays and occasionally, making notes in a dog eared little book. One of the other security guards told me he used to be a big noise in the science world and helped to decipher some ancient language. He got some sort of big science prize for that and wrote several books about various ancient middle eastern cultures.

It was precisely eleven twenty two when it happened. Funny how I remember the time so vividly but I had just looked at my watch to see how long I had until I could take my lunch break, when less than ten seconds later, life changed for everyone. I got a call on my walkie talkie that some woman had become separated from her little kid, a girl of three named Loreen Smallwood. She was wearing a bright red sweater, white pants and had dark brown hair. We all got the call to look out for her, and no doubt the doorman was busy checking the street outside. I had just turned to exit from the Troy Room, when I saw her up ahead of me, skipping along towards the orphan's room. I radioed to the desk that I had seen her, and gave chase. By the time I entered the orphan's room, she was nowhere to be seen and I cursed silently and looked at my watch. I was hungry and ready for a break. As I looked up, I saw her standing by a big stone known as The Tablet of Sondal Dar. As I walked towards her, she stepped forward and ducked under the rope barrier.

"Loreen," I called as I ran towards her. "Loreen, don't touch it hunny. Mummy is looking for you."

I was close when it happened, so close I was seconds away from avoiding the worst disaster in human history, but the kid was faster. So often since then have I wondered if maybe I had been faster on my feet or more alert, maybe it wouldn't have happened. I guess I've always felt responsible, even though I now know it was just a matter of time before someone else did it. Hindsight is wonderful isn't it? Anyway, the Tablet of Sondal Dar is covered with pictographs, in the middle of which is a hand print carved into the stone itself. The pictographs show people running from what look like big humanoids with pointy heads and sharp spears who look like they're slaughtering them by the thousand. No one knew what the stone was supposed to depict. nor which ancient culture it came from, and what little they had been able to decipher, seemed to indicate that it came from, or mentioned, a place called Sondal Dar. Anyway, this little kid, Loreen Smallwood, reached up and placed her hand in the carved hand print before I could reach her. My hand was less than six inches from grabbing her away, but she got there first and giggled as she reached up her arm to the hand print.

The next thing I remember is a blinding light and a searing pain that seemed to split my head in half. I remember screams and running feet, glass breaking and then darkness descended upon me as I passed out. I don't know how long it was until I regained consciousness, but it must have been a few hours, as it looked like late afternoon judging by the light outside. The museum looked like a bomb had hit it, all the windows were broken, the glass cases containing the smaller and valuable items were smashed and the artifacts strewn around the floor. Bodies lay everywhere and many of them looked like they had been attacked by animals. Faces were bitten off, limbs were missing and many had been disembowelled. When I could stand, I called on my walkie talkie and heard groaning in reply. Eventually the groaning identified itself as Charley, my colleague and drinking buddy on our nights off. He was down on the ground floor so I made my way through the chaos and we met by the ticket desk. To my surprise, the old guy, Professor Halpern was with him and looked unhurt.

"What the fuck happened?" I asked and Charley shrugged.

"I was hoping you could tell me," he replied as he wiped blood from his temple and winced.

"I was just collecting that lost kid from the orphan's room when there was this blinding light and pain," I explained. "Then I must've blacked out."

"Excuse me gentlemen," the Professor cut in. We both looked at him. "You were on the third floor weren't you? The Middle Eastern floor?" I nodded. "Tell me exactly what happened prior to blacking out. Exactly mind, don't leave anything out, no matter how trivial."

"Well um," I scratched my head and thought back. "The little kid got separated from her mother and I saw her on the third floor, running down the corridor between Troy and the Orphan's Room. I gave chase and found her at the Tablet of Sondal Dar. She ducked under the rope and reached towards it. I made a grab for her but she was too quick and got her hand into the hand print carving on it. Then all I can remember is a blinding light and a searing pain before I blacked out. Sorry."

"Aha," the Professor nodded, "I knew I'd seen them before somewhere."

"Seen what?" Charley and I replied together.

"I've always been convinced that the Tablet of Sondal Dar is from some very ancient Mesopotamian culture. One further back than any we know of currently. Those creatures that appeared, I recognised them from somewhere and now I remember where. It was an old illustrated manuscript about Mesopotamian beliefs and spirituality. There was a legend of fearsome giant humanoids who descended upon the earth and hunted the people to extinction, but everyone assumed it was nonsense or that it had been wrongly translated. There was said to be a stone gateway that gave them passage from wherever they come from, to here, and that this gateway could only be opened from this side, by the hand of an innocent. When that child put her hand into the carved hand print on the Tablet, it opened the gateway and let them in."

Charlie and I looked at each other and I knew he was coming to the same conclusion as I was, the guy was nuts.

"That's crazy," I sighed and almost laughed. "Creatures? What creatures? It was then I remembered how most of the bodies had suffered horrendous damage, much worse than a bomb would cause, and my resolve at his mental state faltered.

"Didn't you see them?" Charley said. I gaped at him and shook my head.

"No. I passed out right after the light and that pain."

"They were at least nine feet tall," he replied. "With weird helmets that went up to a point at the top and shiny silver armour over their bodies. Each of them carried a spear that shot a beam of some sort and when they killed people, they ate them. It was horrible, just horrible," he gasped and burst into tears.

We stood, without talking for several minutes. Each of us was trying to take in the information and each of us was failing miserably to comprehend what had happened.

"Where did they go?" I asked eventually.

"Outside into the street," Charley replied. "There were hundreds, thousands of them. They just swept down through the building and out into the street, killing and eating as they went. It took ages for them all to exit the main door. We fired on them but our guns didn't have any effect at all. Guss was halfway down the stairs from the first floor and was firing at them, just like the rest of us were. This one creature turned and yelled something at him, and then pointed that spear thing they carry. A beam shot out of it and Guss exploded. His head landed across there by the soda machine, and that's his right arm over there," he pointed to the floor ten feet to our left.

"Did you hear what the creature said when he yelled?" the Professor asked. Charley shook his head.

"Well I heard but I couldn't understand it. It was some foreign language it was speaking."

"But can you remember any of it all, even a couple of sounds might help," the Professor urged.

"Well, there was something that I recognised as Sondal, and then something that sounded like Garrrrrrr. Like an animal growling."

"Well at least that confirms they originated from the Tablet," the Professor nodded.

"Come on," I suggested. "Let's go see outside and call for some help."

That was five months ago. They swept through the city, killing as they went and some people say their numbers increase as they feed. Apparently, there's a rumour that they can split themselves in half and make two of each one, but that might just be talk. The last TV broadcast I caught, said that similar creatures had appeared at several other sites across the world at the same moment, eleven twenty two in the morning. Museums saw them appear from artifacts stored in basements, and several Middle Eastern cities reported them appearing from caves and out of the desert. There doesn't appear to be any way of killing them and we fear that we are to be wiped out altogether soon. I guess it won't be long. I tagged along with some soldiers I met and we made our way across country to Washington, where we tried to put up a fight but they cut through our defences effortlessly.

"So that's how you ended up here huh?"

"Yeah," I replied, coughing and spitting the blood from my mouth. "I'm sorry buddy, I feel responsible y'know? If only I'd gotten to the kid sooner, this wouldn't have happened." I looked across at the old man and knew death was close. The stone pillar that pinned us both to the floor had cut him almost in half across the waist.

"Don't beat yourself up about it Son," he gasped. "If it wasn't that kid, it would've been another kid next year, or another one the year after. Thank you for being here with me by the way, no one wants to die alone huh?"

"Do you believe in an afterlife?" I asked him suddenly.

"Yeah," he nodded. "Yes I do. Do you?"

"I don't know," I replied. "I hope so. It would be nice to think we meet up with folks we've loved, family members and go somewhere to some other life. Maybe we'll be born again when people have evolved on the Earth again. What do you think of that huh?" I looked across but my companion had died and I was alone as I waited for death. Human life was coming to an end and I felt responsible, and yet, death still eluded me as I lay there in agony in the ruins of the White House.

"Thanks for listening Mr President," I whispered to the body next to me, "and Happy Christmas."

THE END

WAITING ROOM
starring Mark Morris & Sharon Rowe

The first thing Mark was aware of, was bright light and a kind voice.

"Mr Morris?" the voice called. "Mark? Can you hear me?"

Mark could hear and before too long he was awake and receiving the biggest shock of his life from the man with the kind voice.

"You mean I'm dead?" he asked, the frown creasing his brow into a deep furrow of disbelief. It took Mark a long time before he could accept the news the kind man gave him, and what made it worse was that he couldn't remember having died. The last thing he could remember was leaving to go to a party with a couple of the guys from work. When the kind man told him that the last nine months of his earthly life would still be a blank for some time, Mark got angry.

"Why can't I remember?" he demanded. "Are you keeping the memories from me on purpose or something?"

"It is your own choice to forget them," the kind man replied, "and in the fullness of time your mind will allow the memories back. Try not to fret about it and just let things happen at their own pace."

"What happens next then?" Mark asked, trying to be practical. "Do I have to go and be judged or something?"

"In time you will have the opportunity to discuss your earthly life and decide how you wish to proceed with your evolution. For now, just try to relax and get used to your new state of being. Another new arrival will be here to join you soon, so you won't be on your own. Someone will come and collect you when the time comes."

The kind man smiled and left Mark alone to explore his new surroundings. It looked like a large airy log cabin, only everything was painted white and there were no windows or doors. The kind man just sort of, vanished into thin air, and Mark supposed that he would learn to do that himself soon. Mark had never been very religious and had always been a little on the skeptical side when it came to ghosts or spirits. He thought of his mother, who had always believed in ghosts and swore blind that she saw her own father's spirit on several occasions, and sent a mental apology to her for thinking she was making it all up. At that moment, Mark heard a distinct ping, and turned to see a photograph of his mother appear on the wall. She was in full colour, the only bright spot in this totally white room.

Nearby, Sharon Rowe was also being welcomed by the kind man. She remembered every moment of her passing and the kind man spent a long time with her, helping her to come to terms with the memory. The pain had been intense, more intense than anything she had previously experienced, but worse than that was the fear. The fear she felt during those last moments changed her in such a way that she would forever be a different being because of it. Sharon felt deep anguish for her parents, whom she knew would be beside themselves with grief at her passing and asked the kind man to send them her love to strengthen them. He promised he would.

"Now Sharon," the kind man said. "Come and meet Mark and spend time together until it is time for you both to continue." She nodded and got up. "Mark doesn't remember anything from the last nine months of his earthly life," he told her, "so don't worry if he seems to be vague about things."

"Where will I go?" Sharon asked as the kind man took her hand.

"Someone will come and collect you in time," he replied. "You will spend time talking about your earthly life and together, you will decide the appropriate place for you."

Mark turned as the kind man re-appeared with a beautiful dark haired young woman.

"Hello again Mark," the kind man smiled. "This is Sharon Rowe. She passed moments before you did and we thought you might like to keep each other company until someone comes to collect you both."

"Hello Sharon," Mark said. "I'm Mark Morris."

"Hello," she smiled back.

Delectus Morbidium

"Don't I know you from somewhere?" Mark replied with a frown. "Your face seems familiar." He looked her up and down and felt a distant memory flutter somewhere deep within himself but stubbornly refuse to surface.

"I lived in London," she said, "in Tooting."

"I'm a Londoner too," he smiled. "I grew up in Wimbledon so we may have met before."

"Perhaps," she replied.

"Someone will come and collect you both when it's time to move on," the kind man said. "You will be comfortable here and if at any time you need me, I will know and be here immediately."

Mark was about to thank him when he disappeared into thin air and left him alone with Sharon. He felt suddenly shy and blushed.

"Feels weird doesn't it?" he said and she nodded.

"Very."

"Do you remember?"

"Yes," she replied.

"Do you want to talk about it? I can't remember a thing and that man said I've forgotten the last nine months of my life. I haven't a clue why that should be and I hate the fact that everything is a blank. I was just going out to a party with some guys and everything goes blank. Most irritating."

"Not just yet," she said. "I'd rather just get used to this, whatever this is." She indicated the room with her hands and Mark nodded. "Everything seems so, so normal. Somehow I wouldn't have expected this."

"I know what you mean," Mark said. "Is this heaven do you think?"

"I've no idea."

"Is this solid?" Mark said as he walked to a large white sofa and sat down. "It feels solid," he nodded as he bounced up and down a couple of times.

"I suppose it's to help us get used to things here," Sharon said. "Maybe later on, things will become more, more," she faltered.

"More ghostly?" Mark offered.

They had no awareness of time passing in the white room, but Mark soon began to realise that he liked his new companion. Once the initial formalities were over, they relaxed and were soon laughing together and sharing childhood memories and the highs and lows of their lives. Without realising it, Mark was becoming fond of Sharon and began to hope that wherever they were to go, they would be together. A few times, he asked her about her passing but Sharon always avoided giving him the details. Mark didn't want to push her to talk about it and guessed that however it happened, it was probably tragic. He put his arms around her and hugged her as she cried. The most she would tell him was that it was painful and she had been very frightened. His heart ached for her and it felt completely natural for him to kiss her and she didn't push him away. His own memories continued to be annoyingly absent and he raged within himself at his inability to remember.

Although not aware of time passing, Mark and Sharon were aware of spending a long time together and of their changing relationship. It was as she was telling him about the plans she'd had for her life, and how sad she was that she would now never get to fulfill them that he told her he loved her as she cried on his shoulder.

"I hope they let us stay together," he said. "Maybe that's why they put us together all this time. Maybe they knew we would fall in love and wanted to give us time."

"I didn't think relationships happened in the spirit world," Sharon said. "What purpose would it serve here?"

"What purpose?" Mark replied, incredulous. "Does there need to be one? We're in love, that's all there is to it."

"I do love you Mark," Sharon said, "but don't be surprised if we don't stay together."

"Of course we'll be together," he replied. "Don't you worry, I will insist upon it."

"You might not be allowed to insist."

132

"If I say we're staying together, then we're staying together," he said.

"Hello Sharon." The voice made them both jump and they turned to see a young man with a determined gaze, standing before them. "I've come to collect you. It's time to go now. Say goodbye to Mark."

"What?" Mark snapped. "Say goodbye? Listen buddy, we're staying together so she's not going with you unless I go too."

"She cannot stay with you Mark," the kind man said as he appeared beside him, "and you cannot go with her. It is time for you to say goodbye now and let her go on to where she needs to be."

"No, I won't," Mark raged. "She's my girlfriend and she stays with me." He went to grab her arm but she vanished into thin air and re-appeared beside the young man. "Come back here Sharon. You're staying with me, don't worry."

"I cannot," she said. She gazed into his eyes as tears coursed down her cheeks.

"Why not? I love you and you love me. You said so."

"I do love you," she replied. "I never stopped loving you and I always will."

"What do you mean, you never stopped," Mark demanded.

"Even through the pain, I still loved you," she said. "Even though I was so frightened and didn't know what I had done to make you that way, I still loved you."

"What are you talking about?"

"You still don't remember?" she asked.

"Remember what? Dammit girl make sense please," he begged.

"Our passing," she said softly.

"Our passing?" he repeated. "I don't remember mine and you've never spoken about yours."

"You were right," Sharon smiled. "We have met before."

"I knew your face was familiar," he replied.

"We met at that party. Your last memory is the night we met. We started dating and quickly fell in love. You were always worried about me cheating on you and didn't like to let me out of your sight for long. The night of my passing, I had been invited out to my cousin's engagement party and despite you forbidding me from going, I insisted. You became angry and violent and locked me in our apartment. I begged you to see things clearly and assured you I would never cheat on you but you wouldn't listen, and couldn't bring yourself to trust me. You beat me to death with a hammer and then killed yourself by jumping in front of a train." By the time she had finished explaining, Sharon was sobbing.

"No," Mark gasped. "You're making this up. This is ridiculous."

"It is the truth my friend," the kind man said. "And when you remember and make your amends, you will be ready to move on. You have all the time you need here and I will always be nearby to help."

"No," Mark yelled. "Look, just get back here Sharon. We can sort this out. I forgive you your little joke, now come here." He stepped forward but the kind man put a hand on his shoulder and despite his best efforts, Mark couldn't move.

"Goodbye Mark," Sharon sobbed. "I forgive you, and I still love you." The young man took her hand and together, they vanished into thin air.

"Sharon," Mark screamed as the bright white of the room started to dim. As the white became grey, Mark noticed a glow begin to seep up from the floor. Yellow at first, it quickly warmed to orange and then red.

"Remember her words Mark," the kind man said. "Her forgiveness is, at this moment, the only thing that is preventing me from escorting you to my domain. Mark turned and looked at the kind man, to see the same red glow emanating from his eyes.

THE END